Northern Hearts

A NOVEL

PAIGE LEE ELLISTON

Revell
Grand Rapids, Michigan

Published by Fleming H. Revell
a division of Baker Publishing Group
P.O. Box 6287, Grand Rapids, MI 49516-6287

Printed in the United States of America

Library of Congress Cataloging-in-Publication Data
Elliston, Paige Lee, 1943–
    Northern hearts : a novel / Paige Lee Elliston.
      p. cm.
    ISBN 10: 0-8007-3161-1 (pbk.)
    ISBN 978-0-8007-3161-8 (pbk.)
    1. Alaska—Fiction. I. Title.
PS3605.L4755N67 2007
813'.6—dc22   2006028883

To Ruth Ann Williams and Paul Bagdon, without whom this book would not have been possible.

1

There must be a million of these awful things!

Tessa Rollins frantically waved her gloved hands in front of the gauze veil that hung from the narrow brim of her hat and surrounded her head. *No, a billion—at least a billion. And they lurk around out here, waiting for me.*

The cloud of Alaskan black flies *was* a cloud, a thick, turgid, slow-moving mass that blotted out the bright sunlight and ebbed and flowed around Tessa's shrouded face. The swirling horde of insects emitted a frantic, sibilant sound that was unlike anything she'd ever heard before.

"Put them good, thick rubber bands around your pant cuffs and your sleeves, or the flies, they'll crawl right on up your legs an' arms, and I'll tell you what: when they take a bite outta you it feels like someone dripped molten metal right on your skin," the elderly woman at the Denali Park Service office had told her. "Some folks, they put wads of cotton soaked in linseed oil in their ears and noses. See, the flies go on in to wherever it's warm and dark to lay their eggs. Thing is, they're really not too bad 'cept for a couple, maybe three weeks every year. Ya know? When they're bad, though, you might want to keep your face covered much as you can."

Of course, I first set foot in Alaska just in time for prime mosquito season—and these flies make the mosquitoes seem like nothing.

Tessa stumbled and lurched to where her university-provided Jeep was parked, her vision, already impeded by the gauze, even less clear because of the fog of insects around her. *For this I left Clearwater, Minnesota? To be carried off by a mass of disgusting bugs? I'm living in a one-room cabin with electricity that works part time and a rotary telephone that ends conversations whenever it wants to. I must be totally crazy.* She clambered into the vehicle and slammed the door.

Then, she took in her surroundings through the scratched and slightly glazed windows, and that made all the difference. *It's a silly cliché, but Alaska takes my breath away. The vastness, the wonderful, untouched purity of it—the exuberance of the land, the sky, the air, the people. I've never seen anything like it.*

The aged Jeep was the boxcar-sized model, a Cherokee. When the odometer stopped working long before Tessa was given the keys, it had read over three hundred thousand miles. Regardless of its age and its battered appearance, the Jeep ran well; the powerful V8 engine purred, and the windows were blessedly tight, which kept the black flies and other insects outside, where they beat against the glass as if in mindless frustration.

Tessa tugged off her hat and its gauze and stuck her tongue out at the buzzing mass outside. She swept her fingers through her shoulder-length dirty-blond hair, turned the key in the ignition, and clicked on the radio. Alaskans, she'd learned, lived by their radios and were never far from them. It wasn't that they were enchanted by the vapid mumbling of the local host or the droning Welkian music he favored. Rather, they were well aware that the Denali National Park Information Service broke into the commercial broadcasts frequently with weather advisories that could be important—not only for warnings about potential storms but also for planned events that Alaskans seemed to love so much, and even the planting of backyard crops.

The Park, as the natives called it, as if there were no other national parks on the planet, encompassed six million acres of the largest state in the union, more than 7,300 square miles of the wildest, most unpredictable, most unforgiving and essentially unexplored wilderness frontiers on earth. Tessa, after slightly less than three months in-country—the native term—still couldn't find the right words to describe Alaska when she wrote home. *Majestic, awe-inspiring, pristine, infinitely beautiful* all sounded bland to her—like describing the Atlantic Ocean as "sizable and damp."

The Jeep's knobby, heavy-duty tires thumped and crunched confidently over the ruts and pits of the access road that led to Tessa's cabin. As soon as the snow started she'd have to leave her vehicle in a three-sided shelter just off the main highway to Fairview and use the old Ski-Doo provided to her as part of her job benefits to get back and forth from her home to the road. She hadn't yet experienced a winter in Alaska, but she'd spent most of her life in Minnesota, where she'd been born, educated, and until recently had taught anthropology at the same university where she'd taken her undergrad and graduate degrees. She believed she'd seen pretty much the worst of weather. The fact that the Inuits had forty-six different words for *snow* bothered her a tad. *Still*, she thought, *snow is snow and cold is cold, whether it's in Minnesota or Alaska.*

The last pile of clippings from newspapers, magazines, and newsletters her administrators at the university had mailed to her shifted forward on the passenger seat as Tessa braked for a cow moose standing in the road fifty yards ahead. The massive animal watched the oncoming vehicle for several moments and then swung her huge head away, apparently more interested in something at the roadside. Tessa tapped her horn. The moose paid no attention. Tessa downshifted, drifted to a stop, and hit her horn again, this time for a bit longer. The moose favored her with another glance; her barrel-sized rib cage expanded with a deep breath that she released in a moment, as if sighing, and then she rather disdainfully strolled into the thick woods on the other side of the road.

The sheer size of a moose had astounded Tessa the first time she'd seen one in the wild, and it still did each time she came across one. The first was an adult male whose span from the left tip to the right of his rack was every bit of six and a half feet. At home a friend of her father's raised Clydesdales, and she knew that a 1,400-pound draft horse wasn't uncommon. That bull moose she gauged to weigh perhaps 1,800 pounds since he stood a good seven feet tall at his shoulder.

Tessa wished she could change her perception of moose in general. *I know it's unfair, but they seem to be . . . well . . . dumb creatures, lumbering around as if they're in some sort of a daze, wandering through settlements and towns like they're alone in the world.*

10

She grinned at the cow as the animal ambled off. "There you go, ma'am—queen of all you survey," she said aloud to the departing moose's massive rear quarters.

The road was clear in both directions, as it almost always was. Tessa still marveled at the absence of traffic, the lack of city sounds, that were so much a part of life in the vast reaches of her new state. She marveled in the same manner too at the string of coincidences and happenstance situations that had brought her here.

At thirty-six and on a tenure path in the department of anthropology at the university, Tessa had found a disquieting monotony to her life. Days were essentially the same; semesters flowed into one another with little to differentiate one from those that followed. Her students became almost faceless, her social life bland but not actually unpleasant. She was alone but not often lonely. Still, she felt a sort of general emptiness.

When the chair of the anthropology department had called her to his office six months ago, Tessa had been both surprised and curious. In his somewhat wordy and more than a little pompous fashion, Dr. Turner had told Tessa that he'd seen her article. She'd written the piece for an anthropology journal on the effects of the twenty-first century on closed cultures, those largely untouched by the modern world. As an example, she'd cited a tribe in the jungles of Borneo whose members, after sighting their first airplane in the sky, began to worship it as a god, to offer sacrifices to it, to eventually attribute to it sweeping powers over all aspects of their lives from fertility to death to changes in the weather. That, Turner told her, brought to mind his correspondence with an anthropologist colleague in Alaska who'd been studying a small group of Inuit people living on the outskirts of Denali National Park. Their way of life had been unchanged for hundreds of generations but was now in many ways in conflict with the encroachment of modernity. It'd be interesting, Turner thought, to "look into it."

Then he'd laid out the string of coincidences to her. The colleague had seen Tessa's article and compared what she wrote to his study in Alaska. The daughter of that anthropologist's sister's minister had taken courses under Tessa and was impressed with her, and that had somehow gotten back to the colleague. He was about to retire and, as an old fraternity pal of Turner's, had contacted Turner about Tessa Rollins—and the offer of an open-ended study of at least one year in Alaska was ultimately made to her.

Tessa had been amazed at how little time and thought she'd expended in coming to her decision. "The Lord's hand is in here somewhere," she'd told a friend. "I know there's such a thing as coincidence, but all this stuff happening in the series that it did, and the fact that I hardly had to think it over before deciding to go—that's more than coincidence." She fully realized that a geographical change wouldn't make her life perfect, and it was unlikely that the nagging little void she felt occasionally would be filled. But, the challenge of the project was exhilarating, and from what she'd seen in *National Geographic*, Alaska was absolutely stunning in its awesome natural beauty. And, she asked herself, *Why not? What's keeping me here at the university beyond habit and a semi-decent paycheck? Shouldn't there be more to my life than grading Anthro 101 papers and being bored to the point of stultification at faculty parties?*

The store appeared quickly, just as it always did. For several miles there'd been nothing but trees on both sides of the road and then—suddenly—there was the general store plunked down in the middle of a cleared quarter acre or so. It'd been built for function rather than beauty—a gray-painted, cinderblock, two-story structure that looked a good deal like a giant shoe box. The parking area in front and to the sides was a rutted and potholed moonscape that tried the shocks and suspension of all but the hardiest vehicles. There was a horse tied to the hitching rail in front, and Tessa slowed to a crawl to avoid frightening the animal. She shut down her engine and read the sign hulking above the store, smiling as she always did when she looked at it. The lettering was crisp and black against a pristine white background, and the whole thing was much too large for the little store. It read:

RUNNING ELK ORLOWSKI'S MERCANTILE EMPORIUM

IF WE DON'T HAVE IT, YOU DON'T REALLY NEED IT.

R. E. ORLOWSKI, PROP.

Even stranger than the store and its sign was R. E. Orlowski himself: a thirty-eight-year-old Wall Street icon who'd simply walked out of his office three years ago and got on a plane to Alaska. He'd sold his penthouse, leaving his furniture, computers, and Armani suits in it, dumped his stock and bond holdings, and began a new life. He'd kept his last name but found his Christian and middle names—Holden

13

Richard—to be modern encumbrances. In Anchorage he'd learned that some of the indigenous Alaskans favored names not unlike those of Native American tribes in the lower 48. The first example of Alaska's wildlife he'd seen had been a bull elk racing across a plateau outside Anchorage. His new name came to him immediately: Running Elk.

R. E. was an open, easygoing sort of guy, easy to be friends with, easy to talk to. Tessa remembered one of their early conversations.

"It takes a lot of courage to do what you did, R. E.," she'd said.

"Courage? Nah. It'd have taken courage to stay where I was, keep on doing what I was doing, until I was too old and too tired to do anything else. That's what I was afraid of, Tess. I would have been fine, I suppose, if I was drawing anything but money out of it. But I wasn't. I didn't hate it—but I didn't love it, either." He thought for a moment before going on. "I don't think God puts us here to be bored with our lives. Not many of us can be astronauts or presidents of countries or whatever, but I think we have an obligation to our Creator to find some joy in the gift of life he's given us, some passion about what we do and where we are."

He was looking into Tessa's eyes, and he grinned. "I can see what you're thinking: how can somebody be passionate about a little general store? It's not only the mercantile, though—it's the whole way of life. And it's Alaska too. I can't imagine living anywhere else in the world."

"Why is that?" she asked, genuinely curious.

His grin turned into a full smile. "Give it some time. You'll see—you'll answer that question for yourself."

Tessa glanced up at the rearview mirror before swinging

the door of the Jeep open. Her hair still showed the effects of the hat she'd worn earlier: a line of compressed strands that made her look like she was wearing an invisible headband. The deep blue of her eyes, however, was vivid and clear. Her face had been often—and kindly—described as interesting, rather than beautiful or classic or any of the other female facial descriptions in vogue. She rarely used makeup beyond a touch of lipstick. Her nose, small and straight and undistinguished, had, she noticed, a red little mosquito bite at its tip. She grimaced and then, after a moment, smiled at her reflection, and the whiteness of her teeth showed between her rather thin lips. *Nice nose, Tess,* she chided herself. *It looks like a beacon. Will it glow in the dark?* She climbed out of the Jeep and tucked her blouse a bit more tightly into the waist of her jeans. Her body, like her nose, was undistinguished, perhaps a bit too thin. Her posture, always erect without being stiff or rigid, made her look taller than her five-foot-eight. She started to the front door, her stride rather long and decisive.

The horse tied to the hitching rail seemed to be almost asleep except for the movement of his long, luxurious tail, which swiped briskly at bugs every so often. His chestnut-hued coat, Tessa saw, was brushed to a fine sheen, and the dark leather of the western saddle was clean, almost polished. She barely noticed the rifle in the scabbard in front of the saddle. Firearms were simply a part of life in much of Alaska, no more noteworthy to natives than the incredible three-foot-long cucumbers, hundred-and-fifty-pound pumpkins, yard-long carrots, and fifteen-pound zucchinis that sprang from the rich soil every summer.

The tin bell over the door rang out its two strident notes

as Tessa stepped inside the store. The place had the feel of a small warehouse—expansive, fluorescent lighted, with stock and merchandise arranged on long, flat tables, on the floors, and hanging from hooks around the walls. There were a few small tables placed near a covey of snack food and soft drink machines and a large aluminum coffeepot the size seen in fire halls and church meeting rooms at the very rear of the building. Tessa stopped and inhaled through her nose, eyes closed. There was a new dimension to the scents here, radically different from that of the stores she frequented in Minnesota: the scent of rain slickers, tall rubber boots, the wooden handles of shovels, hoes, and rakes, the tang of gun oil, the masculine, metallic odor of hammers and wrenches and come-alongs and hatchets and long axes. The myriad goods and supplies of the Alaskan frontier had their own aroma. An open wooden barrel filled with twisted dark-brown strips of moose and caribou jerky added a sharply spicy presence to the air. Tessa inhaled again.

"If I charged you for sniffing, I could retire in a month." The voice was masculine, low, with the slightest residual raspiness of a cigarette habit dropped four years ago. Tessa turned, already smiling.

R. E. stood at her side, slapping dust from his hands on his jeans, his smile broad, his crisp blue eyes focused on her as if she were the only other person in the world. He stood a solid six inches taller than Tessa, but even standing close to her, he didn't seem imposing. His hair, tied back in a neat ponytail, was ashy brown, thick and healthy. He was slim but not gaunt, and the muscles in his forearms revealed by the rolled-up sleeves of his flannel shirt were hard and defined. He smelled very lightly of Aqua Velva aftershave.

"Hi, R. E.," Tessa said. "Do you have time for that cup of coffee you called me about?"

He looked to the rear of the store at the empty tables. "I dunno," he said. "It's pretty busy back there. Do you have reservations?"

"Yeah, I see it's jammed up. But, you *own* the place."

"Well, there's that, of course. I'll talk to the headwaiter, see what I can do."

As they started toward the back of the store, a voice reached them from the far corner where the horse goods were displayed. "R. E., are these the only bits you have?" The boy—a young teenager—wore a pure white Stetson, a leather vest, and western boots. His hair, coal black and lustrous, contrasted with the almost amber color of his skin.

"Yeah, Daanlah. For now, anyway," R. E. answered. "But I've got a big order coming in from Bristol Bits in Texas that should show up any day now—snaffles, cutting horse, high and low port, some of the showy silver stuff too."

"Great," the boy said. "I'll wait." He paused for a moment. "Uh—R. E.? Remember I told you I'm going by Danny now? I'd really appreciate it if you'd . . . ."

"Sorry, Danny. I won't forget again." R. E. pulled a chair out from a table for Tessa and continued on to the coffee urn. When he returned, he carried two old-fashioned ceramic mugs—the thick, heavy ones used at roadside diners—and set one in front of Tessa. She sipped appreciatively. Good coffee, she'd learned, had much the same cultural importance in Alaska that fine wine had in France.

17

"So," she said, setting her cup down in front of her, "what's up? You sounded excited on the telephone."

"I guess I was—am. A guy I met a year or so ago called me this morning. Kalluk is his name—he's a native Alaskan, an Inupiat, originally from the north shore."

"Seems to me I've heard that name, but I'm not sure where."

"Probably from me. I think I mentioned him after the service a couple Sundays ago. He's a native advocate—and a strong one. He speaks all over the place about the rights of the People and how their way of life is being stepped on by the oil conglomerates, corporations from the lower 48, rampant technology, all that."

Tessa smiled. "Almost every indigenous group I've ever studied referred to themselves or were referred to by anthropologists as the People, and each seems to believe that they initiated the term."

R. E. chuckled. "I suppose that's true. The thing is, it sounds *right* coming from Kalluk. He's the real thing—a ton of charisma. He knows his stuff too. He's studied the People's various cultures—and not from textbooks, either. He's lived all over Alaska, hunted, fished, whaled with natives."

"He sounds like an interesting guy."

"He is that. And he's coming here in a couple of weeks for some kind of conference with the Park Board of Administrators." He paused and drank coffee for a moment, but it was clear to Tessa that he was far from finished with what he had to say.

"I hope I get to meet him," Tessa said.

"That just might happen, Tess," R. E. said. "I told Kalluk about you and your study and how you're having a tough time getting things rolling, how your contacts haven't yielded much as yet."

"It takes time," Tessa said somewhat defensively. "Some of the data I've been able to—"

"I know, I know," R. E. said. "But listen to this: Kalluk is tentatively planning a trip of a few weeks or longer into Denali to meet with the People and to gather information about the poaching of wolves and bear that's been going on—not the subsistence harvesting by the natives, but the commercial hunting that's messing up the ecological balance, the migratory patterns of the animals, and so forth. And get this, Tessa—a main thrust of his expedition is to determine what effect all that is having on the traditions and ways of life of the folks out there."

"Wow," Tessa breathed. "I have to spend some time with this Kalluk, both before and after his trip. The sort of perspectives and data he could offer would be absolutely invaluable to what I'm doing."

R. E. sat back, smiling broadly. "That's what I thought. And guess what? Kalluk was interested in your work—very interested. He more or less offered to take you along when he goes into the scrub. And, well, if that works out, I figured I could go along too. Getting someone to run the store here would be no problem at all."

"But a field trip isn't really a vacation, though. Why would you want to . . ." She let the sentence drop to silence, hearing how dubious her voice sounded.

R. E. was quiet for a moment. "Why would I want to go out into the boonies?" he asked. "For the same reason I left New York City and came to Alaska."

"I'm sorry; I didn't mean it the way it sounded. I really

19

didn't. It's just that a trip like that is a major undertaking, and I haven't even met the guy who's putting it together." She smiled across the table. "I gotta admit, it's an intriguing—"

The tinny-sounding bell over the mercantile's door clinked its two notes. R. E. looked over Tessa's shoulder toward the front of the store. His face tightened, and he stood up from his chair. Tessa turned to see who'd entered.

The customer was tall, his skin a bronze hue. His hair, lustrous black, was perfectly straight and hung well below his shoulders. He wore a leather vest over a flannel shirt. The vest didn't completely conceal the butt of a huge pistol in a holster at his waist. "Yo, R. E.," he said, his voice friendly and slightly hoarse. "I come to give you 'nother chance to trade with the natives."

"I trade with the People every day, Taliri, and you know it. But I won't sell ammunition to you or the outfitter you work for. I made that clear the last time you were in here."

The man's voice remained calm, even affable. "You want us to hunt like we were in the lower 48—abide by their stupid seasons and quotas an' whatnot? This ain't New York, R. E. You want us to give up our traditions, our livelihoods?"

"No, I want you to stop leaving moose and caribou meat to rot so one of your mighty hunters can take home a good rack to brag about at the country club. I want you to stop hunting wolves from airplanes. I want you to quit poaching in Denali. I want—"

"You don't sell me ammo, I'll get it somewhere else. But I like to spend my money locally, keep the economy movin'. You make that impossible." Taliri's voice had changed. It was now mocking, and the heat in his polished ebony eyes indicated the taunting wasn't anywhere near friendly.

"Fine," R. E. said, his voice level. "Do what you have to do. I don't need your business, and I don't want your business. Don't come back, Taliriktug. Keep out of my store." He took a couple of steps toward the counter. The other man stood for a moment, glaring. Then, he waved a hand dismissively, as if shagging away a pesky fly, and turned away. The bell sounded again as he opened the door.

R. E. walked back to the table and sat across from Tessa. He breathed out a breath that sounded like he'd been holding it. "Sorry," he said. "I get kind of . . . upset with some of those gun-happy jerks who call themselves outfitters."

"I noticed. Who was the guy?"

"His name's Taliriktug—means 'strong arm' in Inupiaq. He's licensed by the state to guide hunters. I know that Fish and Game would love to yank his ticket, but they can't seem to catch him when his hands are bloody. His clients bring more scotch with them than they do hunting skills, and Taliri makes sure they get to blast away and kill something each trip."

"That's awful. I'm glad you don't deal with him, R. E."

"Yeah. Thanks. The thing is, he's right. He can drive a few hours and buy all the ammunition his truck can carry."

"You can't control that, but you did the right thing." She paused. "What about that pistol he was carrying. Is that legal?"

R. E. smiled sadly. "You really *are* new here. That's a .44 Magnum—powerful enough to drop a mature moose with a single shot. He might just as well haul a bazooka around. But yeah, it's completely legal. Carry permit restrictions were done away with in Alaska, except for in airports and so forth. Guns in vehicles, houses, pockets, purses, just about anywhere, are now perfectly legal."

Tessa began to speak, but R. E. held up his hand, asking for a moment. "It's not that I'm anti-gun. I don't know anyone—native or lower 48—who lives here and doesn't have some sort of a firearm at home. Away from the big cities, Alaska is still a frontier. The animals can be dangerous—owning a gun makes sense."

"You don't have a gun."

R. E. shook his head. "No. There's nothing in the store that I care enough about to get in a shoot-out over, and I live right up above. It's unlikely that a bear is going to climb the steps to the second story and come to get me." He laughed a bit, and the stiffness left his shoulders. "'Course, it'd be a lot easier for a thousand-pound grizzly to get to you in your cabin, but I've given up trying to get you to take a shotgun and a box of shells home with you."

"Good—that you've given up, I mean. I wouldn't know how to use a shotgun, and I don't want to learn. And R. E.—I've told you how I feel about guns."

"Yeah," he said quietly. "You have. I can't say that I really disagree with your feelings." He paused for a moment. "Still, we use tools for what they are, no? And guns are . . ."

"Right," Tessa said quite seriously. "And it's a well-known fact that there's no difference at all between an Uzi assault rifle and a wallpaper glue brush—they're both just tools."

She caught R. E. completely by surprise, and the tension of a few moments ago was washed away by his laughter. "There's no sense in arguing with you," R. E. said with a chuckle. "Every time I try to make a point . . ."

The ringing of the telephone at the front counter brought R. E. to his feet. He held up his index finger to indicate he needed a minute and hustled across the floor to answer the call. Tessa watched him as he moved. She'd noticed right from her first days in Alaska that there was a certain manner in which the native people—both men and women—walked and moved about doing the things that people do every day. There was a grace to them, a quiet ease in their strides, in the way they used their hands while speaking, the way they carried their bodies. It was, she believed, completely unconscious, perhaps even genetic. It seemed to her that R. E., perhaps through some strange osmosis, was becoming a native Alaskan and that his body had picked up its cues from the people he'd befriended.

She watched and sipped at her coffee as R. E. talked on the telephone. A few of his words reached her; he sounded excited, and he was smiling as he looked across the store at her. He hung up and came back to the table, looking like he'd had some very good news. "That was Jim Mickelson from the Park," he said. "There's a good-sized herd of caribou that has moved out onto the plateau near Potter's Divide, and Jim said there's a bull that's really magnificent. I'm sure not doing any business here, and it's not a long drive. What do you say, Tessa? Wanna go and check out the herd?"

"You bet I do! I'll grab my camera from my Jeep while you lock up the store." It was understood without being stated that R. E. would drive. His Dodge Ram pickup with its four-wheel drive, powerful V8 engine, and five-speed manual transmission still smelled new inside, and it was perhaps the only physical possession he had that he was proud of and quite thoroughly enjoyed.

As Tessa opened her glove compartment she heard the throaty rumble of the Dodge's engine from the other side of the building. She smiled to herself: she knew what was coming next, and it did. R. E. revved his motor several times, making the tone of the fiberglass-packed mufflers rise from a low grumble to a manic snarl. R. E. pulled around the back of the store, stopped next to Tessa's Jeep, and revved his engine again. She climbed up into the passenger seat, slammed the door, and worked the shoulder belt into place. She sniffed the air in the cab appreciatively. "Still smells brand new," she said.

R. E. nodded proudly. "I never had a vehicle in New York City, and never wanted one, either. Parking would have cost me better'n two hundred a week, and any decent car would have been ripped off by the chop shop punks, anyway. But here . . . well . . . this truck is something, you know?"

Tessa settled into her leather bucket seat. The sun striking the highly polished black lacquer of the hood made her squint against the glare. "Potter's Divide is right at the periphery of the Park, isn't it? Is there a town or something there?"

"Yeah," R. E. answered. "It's right on the boundary. I guess there was some sort of a settlement there years ago—people mining the streams, panning for gold. There are different stories about the place. I heard that cholera got most of the miners. Hard to tell what really happened. It could be that there just wasn't enough gold to keep the people there."

They rode in companionable silence for a time, the omnipresent radio murmuring in the background, the announcer's words too quiet to register and the insipid music not worth listening to. As R. E. downshifted, slowed, and turned off the paved road onto what looked like a wagon trail, Tessa sighed. "I forgot my hat and gauze. The flies will eat me alive."

"No, they won't. You'll be OK. There's no standing water—no breeding places for the bugs. Potter's stream runs fast and hard downhill from the foothills in Denali. And I'll tell you what—it's snow runoff and it's cold enough to make your well water seem like a cup of hot tea. How those miners kept their hands in it a dozen hours a day or more is beyond me."

"You've been up there before, then?"

"Oh yeah. When my store was being built I had lots of time to poke around and explore. I had an old Inuit with me who charged me for his time in cigars and cigarettes. He'd say maybe three words a day, directing me with his hands and grinning away like he'd just won the New York lottery. Neat ol' guy."

"Cigars and cigarettes?" Tessa asked dubiously.

"Yep. Lots of the old-timer natives formed a kind of instant addiction to tobacco. These days the young people are bright enough not to smoke, but they're a new genera-tion."

The trail rapidly deteriorated to an almost indiscernible rut punctuated by gaping potholes and random large rocks pushed to the surface by the heaving of the land during the spring and summer. R. E.'s pickup sat high on its frame, and the exhaust system, transmission, and other drivetrain components cleared the obstacles easily. The terrain began to rise, at first hardly noticeably, but within a few hundred yards quite sharply. When the angle of the climb made both Tessa and R. E. nervous, he stopped, pulled on the emergency brake, and shut off the motor. "Time to hoof it," he said. "The plateau is just beyond the top of this grade." After a moment he added, "I think."

25

They walked easily together, keeping pace with one another, both struck almost wordless by the sheer beauty of the land through which they trekked. The day itself was stunningly clear, and the sun, powerful but benign, warmed them comfortably, but the intense heat of the summer was gone for the season. The air, moved by the slightest of breezes, was a sensory delight, carrying the scents of fertile soil, grass, rushing water, and the woody, natural smell of the low scrub brush as they hiked through it. *If I had to go back home today,* Tessa thought, *I'd still have this memory with me for the rest of my life.*

They stopped and stood silently on the edge of the vast plateau. The small herd of caribou, made up of perhaps a dozen or so animals, was a half mile distant. The animals were at ease, not clustered tightly, and a few of the cows had calves at their sides. A bull stood twenty yards away from the others, muzzle pointed to the sky, tasting the air for the scents of predators.

"C'mon," R. E. whispered. "We can get closer. The breeze is coming from them to us. They won't catch our scent." He tugged at her sleeve lightly and moved ahead. "Watch that big bull. He's the lookout. Try not to move when he looks in our direction."

The herd continued to graze. As Tessa and R. E. moved slowly toward them, the bawling of the calves and the snuffling grunts of the cows reached them. A pair of cows argued briefly, snorting, posturing as if readying to charge. The bull swung his massive head to them, not unlike a schoolteacher glaring at a pair of fractious children, and the arguing stopped. The cows went back to tearing up mouthfuls of lichen, their differences apparently forgotten.

R. E. was headed toward the cows. Tessa stopped. She shook her head as he looked at her and mouthed the word *bull*. R. E. nodded and changed direction, letting Tessa lead him by half a step. Their progress was almost strobe-like—a half stride before all motion was frozen, then another step, and then another. When the bull shook his head nervously and stared directly at them, they stood statue-still for what seemed like forever. When the animal lowered his head again, both Tessa and R. E. released breaths they hadn't known they'd been holding.

He was a magnificent specimen of the adult male caribou, five feet tall at the shoulder, weighing perhaps seven hundred pounds, with antlers that were at least five feet wide at their outer reaches, and a coat that was a dusty cinnamon hue with a brilliant white neck and rump and splashes of white above his hooves. His eyes, even at a distance, were large and wary, a liquid black.

Tessa stopped, and R. E. halted silently next to her. The bull was showing signs of nervousness—swinging his head, pawing at the ground with a hoof every so often. The smell of the herd reached them on the breeze, a heady, strong aroma of hair and flesh and manure that wasn't at all unpleasant. It was, Tessa thought, the natural scent of Alaska. Never in her life had she seen such wild and natural beauty, never had she inhaled air so pristine and pure, never had she experienced such profound natural silence in which the sounds of animals and the sloughing of grasses in the breeze replaced the noise of civilization.

Tessa's prayers throughout her life had been unplanned and unstructured—neither rote recitations nor solely pleas for help in troubling times. Rather, her worship was of the

27

conversational sort—a dialogue with the Lord. Now, her internal voice spoke: *Thanks so much, Lord. Why you've put me here in this marvelous place is a mystery to me just now, but I'm grateful that you did it—and I know that good will come from it. You take such wondrous care of your children . . .*

Something—perhaps a shift in the direction of the breeze carrying the scent of the two humans toward the herd—startled the bull. He snorted loudly, and the heads of all the cows snapped toward him like the heads of recruits when their drill instructor calls them to attention. The cows stared dumbly at their leader, some of them with branches of lichen trailing from their mouths. When the bull began running, the cows followed him. He led them a couple of hundred yards and then swung back to goad the stragglers into a hard run. In moments the herd reached the line of spruce trees to the west and disappeared into them.

"Magnificent," Tessa breathed. "Absolutely magnificent."

"If I ever get to wondering why I moved to Alaska, I'll watch something like we've just seen again and I'll have my answer," R. E. said.

"That's funny," Tessa mused. "Of course, I don't know you well yet, don't know what makes you tick, but I've never thought—never even considered—the idea that you'd ever leave Alaska."

They walked a few steps back toward where they'd left the truck before R. E. responded. "By lots of standards my life in New York City was a very good one, but it somehow never worked for me. The men and women I knew saw things—life—entirely differently than I did. Money was the prime mover, and possessions were the reason they all gladly put in twelve- and fourteen-hour days. It worked for them, but it didn't work for me."

They walked on in silence amid the velvety pre-dusk colors that seemed to soften all the sharp edges in nature. R. E. was quiet for a long moment and then spoke again. "I think the world in the lower 48 was too fast for me."

Tessa didn't answer, at least not out loud. *At times I think it's too fast for me too. But this is the twenty-first century. We either move with the world or we get left behind.*

There was just enough light left to make visible an eagle soaring through a long arc far above them against the muted pastels of the sky. The bird flew without effort, riding the air currents, wings barely moving.

Tessa watched the eagle's flight and smiled.

R. E. broke the comfortable silence on the trip back to the mercantile. "I've been wondering," he said, but then let the thought and the sentence dwindle to silence.

"Wondering what?"

"Well, you've been here for over two months now, but I'm not sure I know what you think—feel—about all of this." One hand moved from the steering wheel in a sweeping gesture. "Alaska, I mean."

Tessa considered before answering. "I need to respond on two separate levels," she said.

"Oh?"

"Yeah. As an academic—an anthropologist—I'm both frustrated and elated. There's so much here, so much to study, to learn, to absorb. I know that to be true because of the relatively few contacts I've been able to make with native Alaskans—the People, I mean. But I haven't even begun to scratch the surface here. That's frustrating to me. I know this sort of thing takes time, that valid contacts are hard to come by, to develop into genuine sources of information, but knowing that doesn't make the waiting any easier."

R. E. nodded. "I can understand that. Patience isn't my strongest character asset, either. But what about the other level you mentioned?"

Tessa's smile was almost as broad as the Alaskan horizon. "I feel like I'm in the Enchanted Forest in Disneyland most of the time. I never realized our earth could be so spectacular."

2

"You're such a treasure, Meeloa. I mean it. If I hadn't found you, my entire project would have been a bunch of guesswork and academic projections and nonsense like that."

The woman on the passenger side of Tessa's Jeep smiled somewhat ruefully. "I'm glad you think so. Now, if you could only convince one of the eligible guys of what a treasure I am . . ." Her thought ended in a sigh.

Tessa took her eyes off the road for a moment to glance at her friend and translator. Meeloa was twenty-six years old with long, lustrous, pitch-black hair that she spent no time on beyond daily washing and brushing but that always looked like a cosmetic designer had just arranged it for that coveted "healthy, outdoor girl" look. Her features showed her Inuit blood, as did the amber tint of her skin. Her eyes were arresting, a bottomless black that sparked with laughter and softened with compassion. Her eyelids canted upward very slightly, giving her face an oriental aura. She'd studied structural linguistics at Anchorage University, a degree that, Meeloa said, qualified her to clean houses, work in a pet-grooming operation, or wait tables to make a living. Fortunately, she'd been spared those professions by serving part-time as a translator for the Denali Park Service. The assignments were sporadic and the money light, but she lived in Fairview and had frequent contact with the People, and those two things were very important to her.

"Well, those guys are pinheads," Tessa said angrily. "A woman like you—pretty, articulate, bright—"

"Aha," Meeloa broke in, "you said the magic word: *bright*. In the minds of the traditional People, a college education is as useful to a woman as a baseball glove is to a trout. And the new generations of the People—at least most of them—don't think much differently."

"That's dumb. Really dumb."

"But that's the way it is. I won't consider spending the rest of my life cleaning fish and gutting caribou and having babies. So, maybe it's not so much the men rejecting me as me rejecting them. Either way, the end result is the same."

"But, Meeloa, there must be native guys in the cities— Anchorage or Nome or wherever—who realize we're in the twenty-first century. Couldn't you . . ."

"Again, my choice. I went to university in Anchorage, and I couldn't wait to put the city behind me. I belong in Fairview, and I'll stay in Fairview."

"Native men aren't the only men in the world," Tessa suggested.

Meeloa paused for a moment. "I don't expect you to completely understand this, but if I marry at all it must be to an Inuit. It's a promise I made to myself. My people are changing too fast, leaving traditions that have endured for hundreds of years behind. Our elders are dying off, and there's no one to replace them. I have an obligation to my blood, Tess." She paused again and added, "Case closed." There was a finality to her tone that told Tessa the conversation was over.

They listened to the babble of the radio as they followed the two-lane highway at a sedate-for-Alaska sixty-five miles per hour. Tessa had quickly learned that the purpose of speed limit signs was essentially to assist Alaskans in sighting their new hunting rifles, and beyond that the signs were uniformly ignored. There was no residual tension left between Meeloa and Tessa after the marriage discussion—they'd had much the same conversation a few times before. The friendship between the two women was a solid one; it could withstand disagreement or stumbles in communication.

"The turnoff is right up ahead, Tess—by the dead tree," Meeloa said.

"Yep. It always seems to sneak up on me." She down-shifted, and the blown muffler of the Jeep rumbled and grumbled like the exhausts of a NASCAR racer.

It was much more a path than a road. Years ago there'd been some logging of the white pines that were dense in the area, but the long winters and the problems involved in hauling the cut trees made small lumbering operations financially unfeasible. Some ruts from the heavy trucks remained, but they were weed and grass choked, and the rocks that had been pushed to the surface at the end of each winter threatened all but the highest or most effectively shielded drivelines and undercarriages.

Tessa threaded her way around the worst of the holes and rocks in first gear. "What about you, Tess?" Meeloa asked. "What are you going to do when this study is finished? Is there a guy back in Minnesota?"

"No, there's no man in the picture. I suppose I'll go back home and take up with the university where I left off. I'll write about my experiences here for the journals, of course. 'Publish or perish' is still very much the rule in advanced education. I'll probably get tenure before too long."

"You don't sound very enthusiastic about it."

"No? I guess . . ." She stopped for a moment and then went on. "It's a good life. It's not what you'd call exciting, but it's what I know, and I'm really comfortable in academia. I suppose it's a kind of sheltered life, but I've never been big on partying or crowds or huge circles of friends. Maybe I'm too analytical, but that stuff isn't me at all."

"Do you think you'll ever marry?"

Tessa grinned. "Gee, Meeloa—go ahead and ask probing, personal questions that embarrass me, why don't you?"

"Oh, I'm sorry. I didn't mean to . . ."

Tessa waved a dismissive hand. "Come on—I was only teasing." She paused again. "I don't really know if I'll marry. I hope so, but I'm not at all frantic about it. Like I said, I'm pretty analytical, and I'll have to be 100 percent sure before I consider a lifelong commitment."

"Well, suppose you met someone here, in Alaska."

Tessa laughed. "Sure. And suppose I become an astronaut and command the first spaceship to Mars."

"Stranger things have happened, you know."

Tessa sighed. "Not to me."

The group they were going to call upon consisted of three women and one man. Each of them was beyond eighty— how far beyond, none of them knew or cared. They were a dour, taciturn lot, self-conscious with the white woman and her questions. In her mind, Tessa referred to them a bit sarcastically as "The Joy Luck Club" because of the rarity of laughter or even smiles among them. They'd been born into the genuine, ages-old Inuit hunter-gatherer lifestyle, and their memories remained keen, and the stories of their childhoods and young adulthoods were the best type of anthropology—living history.

The three women were sisters; the man was a cousin. They were too old now to move with the seasons and lived in a small cabin left behind by the loggers. Each of them readily admitted, as if it were a casual thing, that they'd have been long dead in the old days. Those who were too sick or too elderly to move with the group were simply left behind. Their language was a polyglot of words and phrases attributed to the Inuits—the people once called Eskimos—and Tessa tape-recorded each meeting in order to study the linguistic structures involved. But more than language, Tessa was interested in their culture, their concept of how groups function together, the leadership within their people, their religious beliefs and traditions, and their vision of their own place in the world.

It was obvious that the elders trusted Meeloa, but they seemed to find it easy to ignore Tessa. Nevertheless, they responded to questions asked by Tessa through Meeloa's translations. In the course of the five previous meetings Tessa had accumulated over eleven hours of recorded comments. Later, Meeloa would translate the tapes word for word.

Tessa initially found it difficult to tell the women apart and had problems pronouncing their names. Their voices were quite similar, and their craggy and lined faces were similar enough that a person could wonder if they were triplets. For the purposes of her study, she and Meeloa referred to the sisters as A, B, and C. The man's appearance was only slightly different from that of his cousins. His hair was shorter although still shoulder length, and his build was stockier, with broader shoulders. His designation was D. The system seemed terribly impersonal and academic, but it worked.

Tessa was unusually excited about this day's meeting. At their last visit two of the sisters had promised Meeloa that they'd perform a bit of throat singing, which was a phenomenon anthropologists talked about but few, other than those who'd traveled to Mongolia, Tibet, or remote parts of Alaska, had seen or heard.

Meeloa's knock on the door of the cabin brought an invitation to enter in a masculine voice in the native tongue. The four elders were seated on a long couch that showed its age by the tufts of stuffing poking through the worn fabric. A blanket hung from the ceiling at the rear of the single room, creating sleeping quarters for the sisters. The man, Tessa and Meeloa learned, slept on the couch. A large black coal stove hulked in the center of the room, cold now but capable of putting out more than enough heat for Alaska's winters. The cabin was clean and tidy, the wooden floor well scrubbed, the few windows sparkling like fine crystal. Two folding chairs were set up a couple of feet apart in front of the couch. Meeloa sat in one, Tessa in the other. Tessa switched on her battery-operated tape recorder and set it carefully on the floor.

Meeloa began with effusive thanks to the elders for sharing their time and stories, for opening their hearts, for their greatly appreciated kindness. It was almost a rote speech, but it was expected as a sign of respect and seemed to put the elders more at ease. Eight dark eyes that glinted like polished obsidian focused on Meeloa as she spoke.

Tessa, as she had at every other meeting, felt that she could have spontaneously burst into flame and not gained the elders' attention. Hand gestures and body language were major parts of the dialect, and Tessa watched her friend's hands and body as she spoke. When Tessa said the word *katajjaq*—throat singing—and ended the thought with a rise in her tone of voice, two of the women rose rather ponderously from the couch and moved to the center of the room. There they hunkered down on their haunches facing one another, about a foot apart. Tessa hoped she'd be able to lower herself with such grace when she was half their age. Tessa and Meeloa turned in their chairs to watch.

The sound was unlike anything Tessa had ever heard before. It seemed to emanate not from the mouths or throats of the elders but from somewhere else deeper inside them. There was a rhythm in the tones and sounds the two women exchanged with one another—while one sang the other rested, and vice versa. The rhythmic motif became louder then more subdued, rapid then slower, but it remained a constant in the singing. The voices were soft, but there was a guttural hint to some of the phrasing; it was music in the way the tolling of a bell is music, clear, repetitive, both sweet and sharp in the air. She felt a strange sensation—a sort of tingling—in her throat as she listened.

Tessa blinked her eyes and leaned forward in her chair. She was positive she wasn't mistaken—one of the women was producing two tones at the same time, distinct from one another yet completely united. The sensation in Tessa's throat became stronger, almost as if she were trying to swallow but couldn't.

There was a hypnotic texture to the singing, and Tessa could feel herself being coaxed into the sounds, the eerie music becoming all there was in her world. The music was a quiet voice that spoke solely to her of the history of the people she was studying, of the tapestry of their love for the land, the climate, the very animals that they both used and feared, of the glorious bands of light that appeared in the skies to gladden their hearts during the endless and barren winters.

The singers stopped together, and the silence in the cabin seemed as strange as the sounds did a few minutes earlier. The two women stared into each other's eyes for a long moment, appearing disoriented and dazed. Then they rose to their feet. Tessa, throat dry and eyes wide, sat staring at the spot on the wooden floor where the elders had performed, her mind chasing itself out of the clouds where it had found shelter. A strangely childlike giggle brought her back to reality. The woman who'd been left on the couch next to the old man was pointing at Tessa, laughing, her teeth bright against the color and the lines and shadows of age on her face.

She's laughing? Tessa thought. *I've never even seen her smile. What's so funny?*

As the singers moved back to the couch, Meeloa asked a long question and received an equally long reply from the elders, who were all laughing now. The old man pointed at Tessa and grinned, just as his cousin had done.

What in the world?

"Your throat," Meeloa explained. "Your throat was moving just like the throats of the singers were. It was as if you were throat singing without making a sound. The elders find that hysterically funny."

Meeloa, Tessa couldn't help but notice, was attempting to swallow her own laughter. Tessa raised her hand to her throat, feeling her face redden with a flush of self-consciousness. Her gaze again dropped to the floor in front of her and stayed for a few heartbeats, until her natural feistiness manifested itself. She raised her eyes and glared at the four Inuits on the couch.

Her glare softened immediately. The eight eyes that had, during several earlier visits, either avoided or ignored her were still as black as pitch but were now suffused with a warmth, a sense of shared humanity.

"And everything changed right in that little moment, R. E. All four of the Inuits were talking at once and laughing and going on so fast poor Meeloa couldn't keep up with them. I got more insight and information in that one meeting than I'd gotten in all the times I'd been there before. And guess what? Next week the ladies are going to prepare a traditional meal for us from salted bear meat and dried roots and things like their ancestors carried with them when they moved with the seasons."

"That's terrific, Tess," R. E. said. "I guess the elders saw that you were genuinely into them and their traditions, and that made all the difference."

"Well, something like that, anyway," Tessa agreed. She waited a moment. "What's bothering me, though, is that I came across as some ivory-tower geek holding a life-form under a sterile microscope and dictating notes full of fancy academic jargon."

R. E. shook his head. "I'm sure you didn't come across that way at all. You don't have it in you to think of people as numbers or bits and pieces of some study. You've got to understand that those elders and many other groups of old folks like them have been plagued by students and social scientists and sociologists and overage hippies who've tried to make the Inuits into a New Age, Back-to-the-Earth, Peace and Love movement. The People don't feel they have to support their traditions by explaining them, and they don't think they owe their time to anyone who wanders by with a notebook or a tape recorder. I've seen lots of these self-styled students, and they're not students at all—they're focused on stuffing the Inuit way of life into the molds of their own agendas." He sat back, looking a little embarrassed at the heat he'd heard in his own voice.

"None of that is what anthropology is really about," Tessa said. "Cultural anthropology isn't an academic exercise or a forum to further a philosophy or belief at all. Our interest is in understanding the ideologies, laws, patterns, and beliefs of the groups we study. It's all about human diversity."

"Yeah, I know that. Meeloa advocated for you to the elders because she knew you wouldn't exploit them. Now, they realize that too."

Several women and a few men came into the store talking amongst themselves. One of the women held a small notepad, and she and the other ladies checked the writing on the page and spread out around the store. The men gravitated toward the display of tools and the Arctic Cat snowmobile R. E. had uncrated and assembled a few days before. It was a sleek, streamlined sled without the boxy look of earlier snowmobiles. The men stood around the shiny, powerful-looking machine just as experienced horsemen would cluster about a fine quarter horse that happened to be for sale. One of the men, Tessa noticed, was holding a brown paper lunch bag in one hand as he crouched and brushed the fingertips of the other hand across the polished black surface of the machine's cowl. The men murmured quietly to one another, their voices like those of people in a church. Tessa didn't recognize the dialect, but they were clearly not speaking English. The fellow with the lunch bag stood and waved toward R. E. and Tessa at the table where they were sitting. R. E. smiled, returned the wave, and stood up. "Guess what that guy has in his bag," he said under his breath to Tessa.

R. E. approached the men and shook hands quite formally with each of them. The man with the bag pointed to the sign on the Arctic Cat that read "$10,449." R. E. nodded. The man spread his arms as if in amazement and shook his head slowly from side to side. R. E. took a half step back and held his hands in front of him, palms up. The old fellow grinned, reached into the bag, and pulled out a banded sheath of bills about an inch thick. Then he reached down and covered the "449" of the price with his hand and gazed expectantly at R. E.

R. E. scratched his head and appeared to be deep in thought. After a long moment he shrugged his shoulders and then nodded, a smile replacing the look of concentration on his face. He extended his right hand to the Inuit to seal the deal. While the two were shaking hands the other men began tugging the snowmobile toward the front door

41

and the truck and trailer they'd left outside. The women had spread their purchases on the front counter, and R. E. walked over to them and rang out the canned goods, bolts of cloth, boxes of ammunition, and the pair of child's boots they'd selected. Within a few minutes the snowmobile and the shoppers were gone.

R. E. pulled out his chair and sat down with Tessa.

"No paperwork?" she asked. "No warranty or registration or any of that?"

"Nah. If the sled breaks down he'll bring it back and expect me to make it right. I will. He'll take good care of the machine. These people aren't much on paper promises. If they didn't trust me they wouldn't come here."

Tessa shook her head in awe. "A ten-thousand-dollar transaction based on a handshake. Whew. I guess I'm not in the lower 48 anymore, am I?" She grinned and added, "After a sale like that, you're not going to charge me for my coffee, are you?"

R. E. looked gravely offended. "Certainly not! It hurts me that you even had to ask, Tessa. For you—today only—coffee is half price."

Tessa laughed but then turned serious.

"What?" R. E. asked, puzzled as to why the smile had left his friend's face.

"I . . . I just don't get you, R. E. You could find yourself in a carload of trouble over that snowmobile. Without papers, there could be ownership issues—liability or something, if that man hurts somebody using the snowmobile. Even here, isn't business . . . well . . . business?"

"No," he said, "at least in my mind, it isn't. Business and contracts and legal loopholes and all that are what I left behind. In a sense, they're what I ran away from, or turned my back on, or however you want to say it. I had to get away from it. It was a kind of life that wasn't working for me—not at all."

Tessa nodded, not quite sure what to say. The intensity in R. E.'s voice was matched by the sudden flare of emotion in his eyes.

He took a breath. "Look," he went on with more control in his voice. "Changing my name might seem like a really silly thing to do, right?"

"No, I don't think that. If you—"

"Please, let me finish. I did it because to me it was a sort of reversal—maybe a negation—of the earlier years of my life. I wanted to make a full break from it, to begin all over again, or as much as that's possible for a guy my age. I'm R. E. now, Tessa. If somebody called out my given name I doubt that I'd respond at all. That guy is gone. And I'll tell you what: I like this R. E. fellow a whole lot better."

3

The wind prowled around and poked at Tessa's little cabin. It created a sad, desolate sound, like that of a faraway train whistle on a dark, cold night. But Tessa felt snug and content. The fire in her fireplace was burning cheerfully, whooshing every so often as a gust twisted its way into the chimney that protruded through the roof. The delightful perfume of the burning aged pine suffused the little building. Summer was a memory, and the autumn season was already nearing its end. Gone with the warmer months were the biting insects, although Tessa still had a few reddish lumps on her wrists and ankles from deer flies. She'd had to settle for dousing them with calamine lotion. Scratching was counterproductive; the more she rubbed at them the more they itched. *At least,* she thought, *the bite on the tip of my nose is finally gone. For a couple of weeks I was starting to feel like Rudolph the Red-Nosed Reindeer.*

Tessa sat at the large table that rested approximately in the center of her floor space. Somewhat rickety, the table was a noble old handmade piece of furniture that she thoroughly enjoyed. The three broad boards that made up its surface were mated together almost seamlessly and showed the marks of hand-planing. The legs were stout and smooth, hand sanded and warm to the touch from their proximity to the fireplace. The surface was adrift in paper: notes, word-processed commentaries, sketches and rough drawings, and reference books from which flocks of yellow sticky notes stuck out like little flags. The twelve-inch monitor in front of Tessa, apparently manufactured in Paleolithic times, flickered almost constantly and was a good match with what R. E. referred to as her "Pre–Civil War" computer. Tessa's multifunction laptop was packed away, battery fully charged, for use in times of power outages, which Meeloa had told her may be in her future, depending on the severity of the winter.

She looked over the sea of paper on the table. It was good work, she knew, solid documentation and tight, logical observations she could support through data gleaned. *Still, this isn't really fieldwork, and there's nothing terribly new or revealing. My face-to-face interviews have been done in a nice little cabin with a mug of coffee in my hand.* Tessa sighed. *I might as well have done all this on the telephone—one of those conference arrangements, with Meeloa translating—from my office at the university.* The beginnings of a smile tugged at the corners of her mouth. *But then I wouldn't have seen Alaska, and I'd never have made a friend of a guy who changed his name to Running Elk and chucked a big-money career to run a little general store in a nowhere town just outside a state park that is larger than the entire state of Massachusetts.* The smile broadened. A replay of a couple of nights ago ran through her mind.

R. E. had appeared at her door with a pair of salmon fillets that would have come from a trophy-sized fish in the lower 48. He looked like a little boy offering a new friend a look at his pet toad; he held the slabs of meat out to her across his extended palms. They'd talked later, after eating, about anything that came to mind: her work, his store, Alaska, the increase of gray wolves in the Park, the fat grizzly that'd meandered through Fairview a week ago with a pair of cubs following her, the 167-pound pumpkin a local native had grown in his backyard garden. It was a good evening, and Tessa had been glad R. E.—and his salmon fillets—had stopped by.

A hollow *thump* broke the silence in the cabin. Tessa listened intently, expecting to hear the howl of a gust of wind that had banged her large plastic trash can against the side of her home. Beyond the light moan of the wind, things were ominously quiet. "Little monsters," she grumbled as she headed to the back door. She picked up the Maglite six-cell flashlight from the shelf next to the door and then, after a moment, the broom that leaned against the wall. She clicked the flashlight on inside with her left hand, clutching the broom in her right, and shoved the door open with her foot.

The shaft of brilliant light focused immediately on three masked faces and three sets of yellowish green eyes. "Get outta here!" Tessa yelled as she whacked at the side of the trash can with the head of her broom. "Go on, ya little bums!" One of the raccoons, in no particular hurry, jumped from the trash can to the ground. Another chewed for a few moments on a leaf of lettuce, his strangely human little paws holding his next treat, a half-eaten piece of toast. His

47

eyes showed no fear—in fact they showed little interest in this banshee with a broom. Nevertheless, he jumped down and stood next to his colleague, both of them eyeing Tessa. The third raccoon joined the first two. Tessa swept her light over them and noticed that they'd arranged a buffet of coffee grounds, pork chop bones, a few stalks of wilted celery, and a series of randomly scattered eggshells. One of the animals, the largest, casually picked up a crumpled Kleenex, inspected it critically, and dropped it back onto the array of garbage.

"Go on!" Tessa bellowed, slamming the broom head to the ground within a foot of the marauders. "Get out of here!"

The animals stared at her for a few moments, as if considering what she'd said. Then, as if by unspoken mutual consent, they turned and strolled off toward the woods. Tessa held her light on the pudgy, waddling rumps and ringed tails and then went into the cabin for a trash bag. As she opened the door, the picture of the raccoon enjoying the leaf of lettuce and holding the crust of toast returned to her. She couldn't help herself—she laughed out loud. To her laughter she added, "If you pests weren't so doggone cute, you'd probably be extinct by now."

The wind had a sharp bite to it, and it carried with it the smell of pine sap from the woods as Tessa gathered up the mess adjacent to her trash can. She shivered as she forced the alleged animal-proof top onto the container and moved it back into its original position. She glanced at her kitchen clock when she came in and was surprised to see that it was almost 11:00 p.m. Picking Meeloa up at 6:00 a.m. wouldn't give her much time for sleep if she continued working. She clicked off her computer and monitor, placed two more logs into the fireplace, and climbed the ladder to her sleeping loft. Mornings, she'd found, came quickly in Alaska.

As Tessa was on the soft edge of sleep, she heard a distinct *thud* against the side of the cabin. She groaned but didn't get out of bed. She settled down again, finishing the final mental words of her nightly prayers of thanksgiving and worship, and drifted off before the next thump came.

In the morning Tessa walked by the second raccoon buffet of the night and just kept going to her Jeep. "It'll be there when I get back," she mumbled to herself. There was a skin of ice in the small puddle left over from the last rain, and it crackled as Tessa walked over it. The wind from the night before had gone on its way north; the morning was piercingly clear and cold, and at 5:40 a.m. the sky was already a vast panorama of cloudless blue. A bald eagle, his seven-foot wingspan supporting his body as if it were weightless, drifted from east to west across the sky, only the very tips of his wings moving as he rode the thermals and searched the ground far below for a meal.

The Jeep started immediately. Tessa turned on the heat, but a blast of frigid air told her to wait until the engine warmed. The Starbucks insulated coffee mug she'd bought in the Seattle airport released vapors of french roast coffee into the cab as she waited for the temperature gauge to nudge itself from "cold." When it did so, she took a long slurp of coffee, set the mug on the passenger seat, and eased out the clutch. The engine labored for a quick moment and then eased as the Jeep rolled forward. The knobby tires, she realized, had been at least partially frozen to the ground.

Meeloa, as usual, was waiting outside her trailer, mug of strong, dark tea in her hand. Tessa had been shivering until the Jeep's heat kicked in, but her friend wore a turtleneck, jeans, and a light jacket and looked as if she were standing in late-May sunshine.

The two women greeted one another with bright smiles.

"I had visitors again last night," Tessa said.

"The night thieves came to call?"

"Yeah, and they scattered garbage all over and then acted like I was pestering them when I shagged them away. This is the third time they've pulled this on me."

Meeloa smiled. "Well, you know what most of the People would have done, Tessa. And, raccoon pelts make—"

"Oh, hush, Meeloa. You know I'm not going to blast them with a thermonuclear device or some such thing. They're just looking for food."

Meeloa's smile spread, and her eyes glinted with humor. "Why not do what some of the fine folks in the lower 48 do? How about a truly meaningful exchange of feelings? Point out to the raccoon that he's manifesting instincts that are natural and wonderful but that infringe on your rights as a person."

Tessa laughed. "You know," she choked out, "my mom always told me that sarcasm is the weapon of a feeble mind. If you can't say something nice about—"

Meeloa continued her tirade. "Open your heart and your mind—your personal aura—to the raccoons, Tess. Explain that although you appreciate and love that the raccoons are releasing their inner children, you feel your cosmic space is being infringed upon."

Tessa struggled to keep laughter from her voice. "Gee, it's great to get advice from a real Inuit—a lady who happens to own an electric can opener."

"It was a gift from my uncle!"

"Doesn't matter. Is your iPod a facet of Inuit culture?"

A young bull moose burst from the trees at the roadside, running hard, tongue lolling from the side of his mouth, chest wet with frothy sweat. Tessa jammed on the brakes and veered to her right to avoid the animal. The Jeep pounded over the frozen ruts that were the shoulder of the road as Tess fought with the steering wheel. The big vehicle responded well, and Tessa brought it to a halt back on the surface of the road. "Whew," she breathed. The moose probably hadn't even seen the Jeep, and in a moment, he was crashing through the scrub and trees on the other side of the roadway.

Tessa exhaled in relief. "He sure was in a hurry," she said. "I wonder what was chasing him?"

"They're moving around this time of the year," Meeloa said. "I imagine he was getting a little porky around a mature bull—probably pestering the cows. This guy looked too young and too small to fight an old bull. It's good for him that he decided discretion is the better part of valor."

"Oh?"

"Yeah. I saw a couple of huge bulls fighting when I was a little girl. It was like watching two locomotives crash into one another at full speed. And the racket! I never heard anything like it—those massive racks slamming together and the grunting and snorting of the bulls. I swear they could have heard the impacts in New York City."

"What finally happened?" Tessa asked.

Meeloa shook her head. "I don't know. My dad dragged me away." She paused for a moment, smiling. "One or the other always backs down—suddenly decides that he isn't really in love with that pretty cow."

The two women rode quietly for a few miles, the low-volume chatter on the radio the only sound other than the creaking and groaning of the Jeep's body and the grumble of its engine.

The elders seemed in good spirits when Tessa and Meeloa arrived at their cabin, and they spoke freely in response to Tessa's questions, often two or three talking at the same time. After Tessa's raccoon invasion and the moose this morning, animals were very much on her mind. She asked, through Meeloa, about the dogs that seemed to be a part of each Inuit family. Even the elders had at least two—half-wild, hulking malamute types that never came close to visitors, had probably never been inside the cabin, and seemed to have no function other than slinking around the area, baring their fangs and snarling at one another and at visitors.

Although their dogs—mostly wolf-canine crosses—were semi-domesticated, the concept of a pet apparently didn't exist in the traditional Inuit culture. The dogs were guards, hunting companions, and working animals and were treated as such. As Meeloa translated one of Tessa's questions with petting and hugging motions, as if stroking and holding an invisible dog, the elders were at first confused and then laughed at the concept. "Does a hunter hold and stroke the spear that is his tool for hunting? The coat that keeps him warm? It is the same with our dogs. We use them and feed them, and it is a fair trade," the man said.

The Inuits served a beverage called zibalsl, a thick, glutinous tea brewed from ground roots and powdered nuts. Inwardly, Tessa cringed. The zibalsl tasted much like diesel fuel smelled and had the same jittery effect provided by several large cups of coffee. To refuse the drink or to leave any of it in the cup was a rather grave social error—not far from an insult to the host.

Afterward, in the Jeep, Tessa belched quietly into her hand. "Whew," she said. "What in the world is in that stuff?"

"I'm not sure," Meeloa answered, "but . . ." She made the universally understood valley-girl gesture of pointing her index finger into her open mouth.

"Yeah," Tessa laughed, "but it was worth it. All that stuff about their dogs and everything is great information." She thought for a moment. "It's strange, though—people so intimately attuned to nature but have no affection for the creatures in their lives."

"That's not the case, Tess. The affection is there, but it's manifested as respect. In a sense, the People see their dogs as important and reliable tools. They take good care of them, and they use them to make their own lives easier. They respect the creatures they eat and wear and make things from too. It's a cultural thing."

"Have you ever considered teaching anthropology?" Tessa asked, not completely joking.

There were still a few hours of daylight left when Tessa pulled her Jeep up next to her cabin. The days were shorter now, though, moving inexorably toward the midwinter period when the sun shed its light perhaps four and a half dim hours out of twenty-four. It didn't take long to clean up the raccoon leavings—after all, Tessa had bagged the results of their first assault last night, and there hadn't been a great deal of anything left in the trash can for their second helpings.

The loudest sound around the cabin was the soft ticking

of the Jeep's engine as it cooled. The peace she'd discovered in Alaska was one of the things she loved most about her new home. Initially, she'd been slightly disoriented by the lack of familiar city sounds. Now she was comfortable with that lack—it'd become the natural way of things.

Tessa wandered toward the line of mature pines fifty yards from her cabin, the ground crunching under her shoes. It had begun to snow, fat flakes that drifted to the earth slowly, as if taking their time to select landing places.

The light in the woods was speckled and scattered by the closeness of the trees and the thickness of their limbs as they stretched to the sky. Tessa inhaled deeply, and the heady scent of the pines flooded her mind with childhood Christmas memories. She looked around and smiled. *It looks like one of those holiday cards with an illustration of a forest and the single word* Peace *under the picture.*

With her eyes she followed the trunk of a tree to the sky to where sunlight filtered through. Not much snow penetrated the foliage, but clusters of flakes seemed to be whirling down directly at her. Tessa stuck out her tongue. It took a few moments before a flake touched down on her waiting tongue.

Tessa began to shiver and reluctantly headed back to the cabin. She'd wrestled two large chunks of a split log into her stove shortly before she left in the morning. By now the little place would be snug and warm. Though the acidic aftertaste of the elders' zibalsl was long since gone from her mouth, coffee didn't seem quite right. But a mug of English breakfast tea would be perfect.

She picked her way back through the forest.

A huge pine, obviously struck by lightning as evidenced

by its burned-out trunk and lifeless branches, had fallen, taking down a pair of smaller neighboring trees. There was dried mud around the base of the large tree, and now a light sifting of snow, as well. Tessa moved closer, wondering why she hadn't noticed the downed trees earlier, since a shaft of fading sunlight served almost as a spotlight on them. Some scratchings in the mud drew her attention.

The pad marks were distinct, as were the punctures in the soil from each of its five claws. "Wow!" Tessa breathed. The distance from the claw marks to the back of the heel measured about eleven inches, and the front pad was perhaps seven inches wide. "Grizzly bear," she said quietly and then repeated, "Wow." Early on, R. E. had shown her the pictures he'd taken of grizzly and brown bear tracks, and a plaster cast he'd made of a grizzly track that wasn't much bigger than the one she was looking at. He also had a foreclaw he'd bought from a native Alaskan. It was about the width of a pencil and a full six inches long and slightly curved to its sharp tip. Tessa crouched over the tracks and put a tentative index finger into the most distinct one. The weight of the animal had forced the pad into the mud an inch or more. She shuddered, imagining the size of this grizzly, and stood quickly. Suddenly dry-mouthed, she peered at the trees and scrub growth around her, quite certain that behind each piece of cover a giant grizzly lurked, hot saliva dripping from its glistening fangs, its eyes brilliant red embers that burned with insane heat. She remembered what R. E. had told her to do if she came across a grizzly or the signs of one: "Don't panic and don't run—but get away. A grizzly doesn't want to run into you any more than you want to run into him—but if that happens, someone could get hurt, and it sure wouldn't be the bear."

Tessa's impulse was to run and run hard. Even though her fight or flight instinct was taking over, she wasn't about to fight a 1,200-pound animal. It took all her self-control to walk rapidly away from the tracks, her mind all the while creating pictures of impossibly huge bears leaping from the trees and onto her back.

When she broke out of the trees and the sanctuary of her cabin was only fifty yards away, Tessa's face was soaked in nervous sweat and she was breathing rapidly—panting—as if she couldn't take in enough air to keep dizziness at bay.

She took a quick peek behind her. Nothing moved in the woods. She turned back and sprinted to the cabin, perhaps running faster than she ever had before in the course of her thirty-six years.

4

The little cabin with its stout log walls and its thick and heavy doors seemed like a secure fortress as Tessa rushed inside and slammed the door behind her. She stood panting and wiping sweat from her forehead with her sleeve, her heart still a trip-hammer in her chest. Around her, her things helped to restore some sanity: the table with her computer and mess of papers, her coffeepot on the stove, her elk-skin moccasins she'd bought at the mercantile a few months ago, the box of corn flakes she'd forgotten to put away earlier that morning, the cheerful fire in her stove that crackled and snapped a welcome to her.

"This is crazy," she said out loud, sounding to herself like a grade-school teacher lecturing youngsters. "I'm in Alaska. I saw some bear tracks. There are lots of bears in Alaska. It's inevitable that I'd come across tracks eventually, and it's equally inevitable that at some time I'll see a live one. Big deal." Her breathing became normal, and the rush of adrenaline that had fueled her frantic run receded, leaving her feeling a little foolish and a tiny bit shaky.

"What a wimp," she added to her soliloquy, grinning a bit now.

Although it was barely beyond midafternoon, the sun was already beginning to weaken for the day, and the light had taken on the dusk quality, the gentle, softening effect coming earlier each day. Tessa stood looking out her front window. The snow had started again, lightly, flakes floating easily, lazily, with no wind to drive them. She moved to her telephone and dialed—not from buttons but with a genuine rotary dial—R. E.'s number. As ever, his voice conveyed his happiness at hearing from her.

"But, Tess," he said, "I have a bunch of folks here at the counter. How about if I call you back in a few minutes?"

"How about this instead: come on over for supper after you close the store. I don't have much here, but I can put something together for us. We can play Scrabble later if you like."

"Sure—and you'll come up with more made-up words like *sard*."

"It's a perfectly valid word," Tessa protested. "Like I told you, it's a little red sort of gemstone. Very popular in India or somewhere."

"Yeah. Right. A little red gemstone. Popular in Tessa Rollins's mind is where it's popular. I ordered an unabridged Webster's from Amazon, and I'm going to keep it at your place. It'll be our final arbitrator."

Tessa barely heard a female voice in the background at the store saying, "I've got three screaming kids out in the truck and I gotta stand here and listen to R. E. and Tess having a Scrabble tournament."

Tessa laughed. "Who was that?" she asked.

"Sudiil. She's apparently feisty today—kinda hostile too. I better get to her or she'll bring those kids inside my store. See you in about an hour, OK?"

"Great," Tessa said. "Tell Sudi I said hi."

Tessa hadn't been exaggerating when she told R. E. she didn't have much food on hand. She scrounged through her cupboards, found a pair of stale Oreos, which she immediately ate, several containers of various spices, four cans of tomato soup, some crackers, and that was essentially it. She moved to the refrigerator. The pickings were lean there too: one egg, a block of cheddar cheese, a somewhat limp looking but not quite ready to pitch head of lettuce, a wrapped half of a tuna sandwich that was ready to be donated to a penicillin factory, a bottle of ketchup, an apple, a half stick of butter, and a plastic bottle of Italian salad dressing. A jar of peanut butter that was down to the scrapings that clung to the inside of the jar stood at the rear of the refrigerator shelf, as if it were a sentry watching over the other paltry contents. What she *did* have was a fresh loaf of homemade bread that Meeloa had baked and given to her, still in its wax paper wrapper.

She sighed. Tomorrow was grocery day—which coincided with her receiving her paycheck—but that didn't do her any good this evening. Her list was extensive; R. E. had told her to begin stocking up for the winter. His arrangement with a supplier to the park service to fill grocery orders for his customers depended upon the weather during the winter months, since the roads were so often impassible.

Tessa closed the refrigerator door and looked back at the cupboard, the door of which she'd left open. She pondered for a long moment. Then she smiled and said, "Aha!"

"That was really good, Tess," R. E. said, pushing his chair back a bit from the table. "Those bits of apple in the salad were a great idea, and toasted cheese has been my favorite sandwich since I was a kid."

"You forgot to mention the tomato soup," Tess said. "I spend the entire day in the kitchen preparing this feast, and you forget all about the soup."

"I was just about to get to the soup," R. E. said. "It was ambrosia—Campbell's absolute finest, perfectly prepared."

Tess stood. "Well . . . OK. Care for coffee?"

"You bet." He stood too and picked up his soup bowl and plate and followed Tessa into the kitchen. "Are you sure you don't want to go out with a flashlight to show me those bear tracks? I'd really like to see them. From the size you described, that guy must have been a giant."

"Like I want to go out in the pitch dark in zero-degree weather with a flashlight looking for a grizzly bear."

"Come on, Tess—he's probably fifty miles from here by now. He was looking for a cave or something to hole up in for the winter, is all."

"Maybe so. But, those tracks aren't going anywhere. Even if they're covered by snow, the ground was already frozen, so they'll be there until spring. I'll take you out there in daylight. You can bring your camera and your plaster-casting stuff too. OK?"

"OK. C'mon, let's drink our coffee on the couch."

Tessa's couch was small and had a blanket draped over it to cover the places where the fabric had been worn through. It creaked and complained when more than one person sat on it, but it faced the woodstove and was near enough to feel the waves of heat from the burning wood, and that made it a fine place to sit.

R. E. sat in the left-hand corner of the couch and extended his legs toward the stove. Tessa sat at the right end and leaned back, sipping her coffee.

"This is nice," she said.

"There's nothing like watching a nice, warm fire on a cold night," R. E. said. After a silence, he added, "You know, it's really impressive the way you've taken to Alaska. If your first winter here doesn't drive you batty, I'd bet that you'll be here forever."

"Oh? Minnesota winters are no joke, and I lived through a whole bunch of them with no ill effects."

"Mmm. It's a matter of intensity, and it's kinda hard to explain. We'll talk about it in a few months and see what your perspective is then. OK?"

"I'm pretty sure I could live anywhere if it felt right to me, if I had a strong enough reason to be there."

"Well, sure," R. E. said. He smiled at her. "I was talking to a cousin of mine I call every so often. He said that when I talk about Alaska I sound like a reformed cigarette smoker trying to convince everyone else to quit. I guess he's right. The thing is, my life has changed so much—it's so much better—that I can't help but attempt to persuade others to do what I did."

Tessa set her cup down. "I guess I know what you mean. It's only logical that when something works or fits as perfectly as Alaska does for you, you'd want others to find the same happiness. But, were things really so bad in New York City? There are lots of business students back at my university who'd give their firstborn to have the job you had."

"I know that. And New York is the greatest city in the world. The theaters, the arts, the restaurants, the various neighborhoods, Central Park with its free concerts, all of that was wonderful. There was always something exciting to do, something to see. And the job—that was fine too. I was good at it. I made a basketful of money for, actually, not doing a whole lot." He sighed.

"What?" Tess asked.

"I'm sure I sound like a spoiled rich kid who wants to run away and join the circus or something, just because it's different. But there's more to it than that. It's like I had this itch, and I couldn't scratch it in New York City, and it was driving me nuts—and I knew I could scratch it somewhere else and it wouldn't bother me any longer."

Before Tessa could reply, R. E. went on.

"OK, OK—I know the itch thing is goofy." He thought for a moment. "I think a hundred and some years ago I'd have gone West to see what was there, to experience it, I guess. I'm not an adventurer by nature, but once I decided to move here, I could barely think of anything else. Maybe it became an obsession, but obsessions are irrational, right? This whole thing wasn't irrational. It's the best thing I ever did."

"Maybe you are an adventurer, R. E.," Tessa suggested. "And I don't think *obsession* is the right word. Rather than running *from* something, you were going *to* something you believed would be better."

There was a silence between them, but there was no tension to it; it was simply a few moments of quiet that left each person to his or her thoughts. Outside, the wind had begun to move, and a gust whisked down the chimney of the stove, creating a flurry of sparks in the firebox.

R. E. hefted himself from his comfortable position on the couch to his feet. "I hate to leave you and this fire," he said, "but I've got paperwork that's calling out to me." He yawned, covering his mouth with a hand. "Yeah, right," he said. "That stuff will wait. What I really want to do is to curl up in my bed and sleeeeeep." He stretched the word as if he were already in bed and dozing off. "Thanks for the meal, Tess. It's been a good night—even if we never got the Scrabble board out."

"It has been, R. E. Thanks for the company and the conversation."

◦•◦

Tessa stood at her window and watched the taillights of R. E.'s truck until they made the first curve in her driveway and were out of sight. A snow squall scudded by with the wind, sweeping whitely across the open ground between the cabin and the tree line in the distance.

She walked to the woodstove and used an oven mitt to swing the door open. The big, aromatic chunk of pine she eased into the firebox would keep her warm throughout the night. She closed the door, watched for a few minutes until tiny orange flames began to pirouette along the length of the new fuel, and went on to the kitchen. She rinsed the carafe of the coffeemaker in faucet water that was so cold it felt like fire on her fingers, and clicked off the light over the window at the sink. As she was passing the little table that held her telephone, a scratch pad, and a give-away ballpoint advertising a record store in Minneapolis, the phone rang. The burring sound was as intrusive and as unexpected as the screech of a chain saw in the quiet of the cabin.

"Tess? I hope you weren't asleep yet, but I just had to call you."

"No. I was just straightening up a bit. You sound excited, R. E. What's going on?"

"Good news. I just now got a call from Kalluk. He'll be here in a couple of days, and he wants to start outfitting right away for the field trip. He wanted to know if you were still interested." When Tessa didn't immediately reply, R. E. went on. "You remember Kalluk, right? The native guy, the speaker, the People's advocate? The guy who—"

"Of course. You just kind of caught me unaware. That's great news. Did he say for sure when he'd be in?"

"He wasn't completely sure. A bush pilot friend of his is going to drop him on that long strip of highway outside of Fairview on his way to a hunter camp."

"Highway?" Tessa was incredulous. "You don't mean . . . ?"

R. E. laughed. "I sure do. It's as illegal as can be, but the bush pilots put down wherever they can, and what makes a better runway than a straight road?"

R. E.'s laugh was infectious. "I see your point. Does this Kalluk travel with a crew or something? For field trips, I mean?"

"Nope. He travels with his dog and recruits folks or goes out by himself. He . . . well, it's hard to explain. You'll know what I mean when you meet him."

"Mmmm," Tessa said, not at all sure how to respond. "Boy—you caught me in my pre-sleep mode," she admitted, "and I'm not thinking too clearly. I mean, if the guy can really put together the kind of field trip you said he could, I might be very interested."

"He can—he does. Take my word for it. I'm really looking forward to it."

"What?"

"Don't you remember I told you I wanted to go on this trip too? That finding someone to run the store while I was gone would be no problem?"

"I didn't forget," she said. "It's just that we haven't really talked about the field trip lately, and I wasn't sure if Kalluk was going to make it here or not. You mentioned that he has speaking commitments and is spread kind of thin with all his activities."

"Yeah. He's always got something going on. But now he's coming, and the trip is going to happen." He laughed. "I've already gotten my camera catalogs out. There's a new Pentax that's pretty expensive. But it's a great camera, and the ads say it works perfectly in any conditions, including subzero temperatures."

"How long will the group be out?"

"Hard to say. Kalluk said he's made plans to hook up with a family of traditional Inuits—natives who live just as their ancestors did, going back generations. He wants to spend some time with them, get some insight into the old ways of the People and determine how all the changes around them affect how they live, how they think."

"Sounds fascinating. Does he videotape or voice-record for documentation?"

"No, that stuff isn't Kalluk's way. Remember, this isn't a study for him the way you'd think of it. He has an amazing ear for language and an awesome memory for detail, so what he learns and sees stays with him. Then, when he speaks to audiences, all that information kind of flows out of him like . . . like a story, I guess. I saw him at a college outside of Anchorage. It was stunning—I mean it. No one moved or coughed or whispered during the entire time Kalluk was speaking. I half expected the audience afterward to go out and burn their cars and hunt seals and bears."

"I sure want to spend some time with this guy." She breathed out loudly. "Oh great, now you've got me all excited, and here it is the middle of the night and I probably won't sleep a wink thinking about all this."

"It's twenty-two minutes after ten, Tess," R. E. teased. "Even in Alaska, that's not the middle of the night." He added, "Of course, if you were still in the lower 48, you'd be just getting ready to go out to dinner to a famous night club with some grand prix driver, right?"

Tessa laughed. "Right. Minnesota university towns are loaded with fancy night clubs and grand prix drivers looking for old maid anthropology professors. They all wanted to talk about crop and migration anomalies in the Basque countries, as I remember it."

"Somehow, I doubt that's what they wanted to talk about, Tess. Anyway, I wanted to let you know what's happening."

"I'm glad you did. Thanks. Call me tomorrow as soon as you find out more about Kalluk getting here, OK?"

"Sure. Good night, Tess."

Sleep to Tessa *did* seem like a remote possibility now. She clicked the kitchen light back on and searched through her cupboards for the herbal tea selection she'd brought from home. "Sleepy Time," in spite of its sappy name, seemed like the best choice, and she turned on a stove burner and put her teakettle over it.

She stepped to the window over the sink as she waited

for the kettle to whistle. She gasped as she looked outside. The northern lights—the aurora borealis—were in their full and magnificent display. A curtain of a pastel-like pinkish red swept across the sky, gently penetrated in places by long drapes of a grayish green mist. Sweeping streams of an electric blue twisted and flowed randomly, like banners touched by breezes. There was only light cloud cover, and what clouds there were—soft cumulus types—took on the hues of the panorama of color, altering the shades slightly, turning them less distinct but somehow warmer appearing, like the glow of a far-off fire seen through light fog.

Having glass between herself and the beauty in the sky seemed somehow profane to Tessa, and she hurried past the stove with its hissing, ready-to-whistle kettle, and pushed open her back door. She stood outside, the air sharply cold and clear, her slippers making the snow squeak and squeal under her. Tessa drifted into the grand and breathtaking array, feeling for long moments that she was strangely a part of it in some inexplicable fashion.

A series of shivers and the clattering together of her teeth brought Tessa back from wherever she'd been and put her back outside a rough cabin near Denali State Park in Alaska in nine-degree weather. When she went back inside her cabin, she discovered that not all of the water in the teakettle had boiled away. The pot shrilled at her as she poured a cupful over the teabag and shut off the stove. She held her cup in both hands in front of her face, inhaling deeply, the warmth of the sweet, grassy, herbal scent helping to chase away some of her chills and shivers. She drank her tea, brushed her teeth in her tiny bathroom, and scurried up the ladder to the sleeping loft. She changed into her pajamas and snuggled into a catlike ball in her bed, tugging the covers close to her.

I can't say being the only woman with a bunch of men on a field trip is my favorite thing, she thought. *But I've done it before, and I suppose I'll do it again in the future. And what a great opportunity the trip is—interacting with Inuits with a native translator and student of the culture right there in camp.*

She turned over, her imagination chasing sleep. *I'd need better boots and some more thick socks. My gloves are silly things, about as protective as the ones my mom wore to church on Sundays. A hat—I'd need a real hat with earflaps. Thermal underwear—that's essential. A good sleeping bag. I still have the sleeping bag I used in my Brownie troop sleep-out. It'd probably cost more to have it shipped here than it would to buy a decent one. Besides, it's pink and has pictures of Barbie on the lining.* She grinned at the image of a tall, muscular Inuit dressed in an elk-skin coat gaping at her as she unrolled her Barbie sleeping bag.

Tessa continued her mental list, feeling foolish for doing so, but enjoying the fantasy nevertheless. *Extra batteries for my recorder. A bunch of tapes. Legal pads and ballpoints. Aspirin. My Maglite and extra batteries for it.* Sleep finally did come. Her last conscious image as she drifted off was of herself struggling across the frozen tundra under a huge load of miscellaneous junk like a grossly overloaded pack animal.

5

Tessa awoke with a sensation of anticipation, almost giddiness. It wasn't only about the impact such a field trip could have on her research and reporting about Inuit traditions—it was also about seeing and experiencing more of Alaska, living with and in the elements, leaving behind the toys and tools of contemporary American living. It would be an adventure as much as a study. But, naturally enough, facets of her academic and analytical side intruded on the excitement she was trying to control. *Suppose this Kalluk is much less than R. E. makes him out to be? Suppose the trip is all talk and won't really happen?*

Even as Tessa admonished herself with logical questions and concerns, the visceral feeling that something exciting—something good—was about to happen stayed with her. She looked out the window over the sink as she rinsed her cereal bowl and spoon.

The day was a radiant one; the sun was finally exerting some strength after the long and murky wintertime dawn.

Now, the light glinted on the pristine patches of snow so brightly that she had to look away.

When Tessa sat at her table, coffee mug in hand, she intended to arrange her laptop files and steno-pad notes into a chronological series, first editing each for accuracy, clarity, and coherent phrasing. It would have been a whole lot easier if she had reviewed the cards prepared on any given day on that day. If she'd done so, she wouldn't be faced with what looked like a Dumpster load of paper rectangles scattered across her work area. She worked assiduously for perhaps ten minutes.

Then she began adding items to the list she'd begun in bed last night.

When a small plane droned by overhead, Tessa looked up, as if she could see through the ceiling of the cabin. Hearing planes buzzing by was certainly nothing new, particularly at this time of the year, when bush pilots were flying hunters deep into the raw interior of Alaska for trophy caribou, moose, and bear. She despised sport hunting. It seemed to her to be a total disregard of life for no real purpose, and the concept of a man with a high-powered rifle killing a magnificent animal, spilling the creature's blood, just to mount its head on a wall, disgusted her. *Barbaric* and *cruel* were the two words she used most often in discussing sport hunting.

She was well aware that the People hunted year round, with no concern for the government-mandated hunting seasons or limits. The Inuits had done this for hundreds of years and, like their American Indian cousins, wasted nothing of their kills.

The sound of the plane had become a distant rumble, but now it was coming back, the rumble rising to a sharp whine

70

and then to the throaty roar of a powerful engine. Tessa hurried to her back door and stepped outside, scanning the sky toward the highway leading to Fairview. The aircraft, a single-engine job painted a bright red with some writing she couldn't quite make out on its side, wasn't much above treetop height and was nosing downward. The pitch of the engine changed to a throaty snarl as the plane dipped below the trees, out of Tessa's line of sight. She stood, hand on the edge of the door, listening, watching. In what seemed to be no more than a quick minute, the engine changed tone again, and the airplane popped up over the trees, climbing hard. In a matter of moments it was a small, silent speck in the distance in the cloudless sky.

When her phone rang forty minutes later, Tessa already had her boots on and was ready to shrug into her heavy coat. She did so as she answered, fumbling the receiver for a second.

"He's here," R. E. said without a greeting, his voice like that of a little boy telling a friend that he'd gotten a puppy for Christmas. "Can you come to the store? I'd really like you two to meet."

"Sure, I'll be there in fifteen minutes."

"Great! Oh, just thought I'd warn you. There'll be a kinda frightening-looking dog out in front of the store. Don't pay any attention to him. He's Kalluk's, and he's perfectly OK."

"What's frightening about him if he's OK? Is he mean or something?"

"Well, no—not mean, not exactly, anyway. The thing is, he looks just like a wolf, except larger. That kind of intimi-dates people."

"But he's an OK dog, right?"

"Right."

"See you in fifteen minutes, then."

Tessa got in the Jeep and pulled it onto the road. *That fits with my impression of the great Kalluk,* Tessa thought as she smiled to herself. *A frontier man of steel who travels with his faithful canine companion.* Her slightly mocking smile disappeared as the thought continued. Although she knew it was quite impossible, Tessa was certain she felt the neat line of long-healed punctures on her right calf that'd been there for almost thirty years. And she could still hear the slavering growl of the neighbor's German shepherd as his teeth cut through her skin. She recalled the bone she'd taken from him, intending to throw it for him to chase, and how the dog had snatched it up from the ground and run off as Tessa screamed in pain and fear. *That was a long, long time ago,* she told herself.

Tessa did her best to ease her old Jeep over the frozen ruts of the mercantile's parking area, but the creaks and bangs of the vehicle made her cringe. She reached out to pat the dashboard sympathetically, considered the silliness of such a move, and then did it anyway.

As she opened the Jeep's door and stepped out, she caught a flash of motion at the corner of the building. There'd been nothing there a second ago; now there was.

Tessa's mind at first told her the animal was a large German shepherd. Even as the thought was settling, she knew she was wrong. Her best friend's family had owned a pair of collies named Hansel and Gretel. But neither Hansel nor Gretel carried their heads like that, sloped down a bit from their bodies. And this dog was too big. His eyes were arresting: motionless, a honey shade of gold with obsidian pupils. The animal stood statue-still, a forepaw lifted an inch or so above the ground.

His coat, heavy and thick, for the most part was a dusky ash color, but his broad chest was pure white. He stood a yard tall at the shoulder. He wasn't menacing—at least not precisely so. Instead, he projected the *possibility* of quick violence, like the aura that surrounds a poisonous spider in a glass enclosure in a zoo.

"Hey, Tess!"

Tessa looked away from the animal to see R. E. standing at the store's door. When she looked back, the animal was gone. She took a step back and pointed to the corner of the building. "I guess I kind of met Kalluk's dog," she said.

"He won't bother you. He can be a little scary if you don't know him, is all. C'mon, let's go inside."

A native woman Tessa didn't recognize sat at a table at the back of the store, her coat draped over the back of her chair, her attention focused on the tall man who stood facing her. The man motioned with his hands as he spoke. His luxuriant ebony hair reached his shoulders. He wore a leather vest over a chambray work shirt, jeans, and black engineer-type boots. His shoulders were broad, and his upper body tapered to a narrow waist. Tessa and R. E. walked toward the table, and the man turned to face them. His eyes went immediately to Tessa's, and for a moment she felt like a butterfly pinned to a corkboard.

His skin was the darkened amber of the older, hunter Inuits Tessa had met—a naturally reddish hue deepened by countless hours under the sun and in the elements. His features were chiseled, without softness, cheekbones high

73

and prominent, forehead wide, eyes chestnut black, nose straight, mouth that didn't seem like it would smile easily.

"You're Tessa, the anthropologist," he said.

"And you're Kalluk, the activist."

Now he grinned, and his entire face lost its hardness for that moment. "At your service," he said. His voice was amazingly similar to that of Johnny Cash, who was a favorite of Tessa's father.

He put his hand on the seated woman's shoulder. "This is Jessie," he said. "An old, old friend and probably the finest paid guide anywhere near the Park."

"Not so old, Kalluk." The woman smiled, revealing white teeth that a dentist would envy. She was, Tessa estimated, in her midforties, with her black hair untouched by silver and cut quite short for a native woman. Tessa took Jessie's outstretched hand. "Good to meet you, Jessie," she said. Jessie's hand was warm and her palm rough with calluses.

Kalluk's hand was extended as well. His palm, Tessa found, felt much like Jessie's—proof that both of these people didn't spend much time pushing papers or punching computer buttons.

R. E. pulled out a chair for Tessa and headed toward the coffee urn. Kalluk sat next to Jessie.

"I saw your . . . uh . . . pet outside, Kalluk," Tessa said.

"That critter is about as much a pet as a piranha would be," Jessie said with a smile.

"He's a good ol' boy—maybe a bit strange the first time you meet him. He'll grow on you."

Tessa nodded. "What's his name?"

She was surprised to see Kalluk's element-darkened face suffuse with blood. *Is he blushing?*

"Well . . . I usually just call him Boy, or You, or whatever comes to . . ."

"Tell her," Jessie said.

"Well . . . you've gotta understand that . . . see, my niece . . ."

"Tell her," Jessie repeated.

He sighed. "His name is Fuzzums, actually."

Tessa couldn't stop the giggle. "Fuzzums?"

R. E. returned to the table and put a cup of coffee in front of Tessa. "What's so funny?" he asked.

"It's not that it's funny," Tessa gasped. "It's just . . ."

"Funny," Jessie said.

"Well, yeah," Tessa admitted.

Kalluk sighed. The blush in his face had receded. "The first place I brought him—right from the folks I bought him from—was my sister's house. My niece was three at the time, and she fell in love with him and begged to be allowed to name him. How could I say no to her? So—Fuzzums it is. He answers to Fuzz or Boy, though."

"That's very cute, Kalluk," Tessa said. "I didn't mean to laugh, but the name was kind of a shock."

Kalluk smiled. "Sure. No problem." His eyes held hers for a moment longer than the situation called for. There was a short, not completely comfortable silence before R. E. broke it.

"So, Kalluk," he said. "What have you been up to since you were last here?"

"The usual. I've been speaking in the big cities—Anchorage, Fairbanks, Juneau—trying to drum up support for my social programs. There's the hunting thing too. Demanding that traditional native groups buy licenses and abide by government-established seasons and limits is crazy. And now this airplane stalking and killing of wolves . . ." He shook his head.

"It's an awful thing," Tess said.

"I'm afraid you'll soon hear more about it. I've been told that lots of it goes on near—and inside of—Denali. They call it 'aerial gunning,' and there's about as much sport in it as there is in clubbing baby seals. These outfitters, as they call themselves, charge fat cats from the lower 48 six to seven thousand dollars for a couple days of murdering wolves from a nice warm two-engine plane with a pitcher of martinis at their elbows." Kalluk's voice took on a hard, sharp edge of disgust. "Sometimes they'll go back for the pelt if the kill was large enough. Most times it's not worth the trouble to them."

"But aren't the wolves protected by the state, by the feds, at least to some degree?" Tessa asked.

Kalluk and Jessie looked at Tess as if she'd just asked if the tooth fairy was real.

"It's a joke," Jessie said. "A sad, cruel joke." There was pain in the tone of her voice. The silence around the table this time was a grim one.

"Anyway," Kalluk went on, "I've spent more time than I ever wanted to listening to car horns and city racket. It's great to be back in the real Alaska."

Tessa wondered why no one had brought up the field trip yet, but she'd learned that the Inuits didn't leap into important topics in conversation. It was considered good manners and respectful of the parties concerned to spend some time in general chatting and local gossip first.

"Where will you stay while you're here, Kalluk?" Tessa asked.

Jessie smiled. "I've booked him in at the Fairview Hilton," she said.

"The Fairview Hilton?"

"Yeah," Jessie said. "I have an old hunting cabin my grandfather built many years ago not too far from your place, Tessa. It has every amenity a native Alaskan needs: no electricity, no running water, a falling-over privy, and gaps between the logs big enough to let the wind and snow inside."

"Sounds swell." Tessa grinned.

"It's not as bad as Jessie makes out," Kalluk said. "And I won't be there all that long." He paused for a moment. "I'm hoping to get the field trip organized and ready to go within a couple of weeks. If I don't, I could miss the connection with the group I want to hook up with."

"R. E.'s told me a little bit about your plans," Tessa said. "I'd like to hear more."

"There's not a whole lot to tell. It was—is—kind of a spontaneous thing. I met the great-granddaughter of an old native who still travels with his family, still lives like his ancestors did. The guy is over eighty, and from what I've heard, he could probably outwork R. E. and me on the worst day he ever had. There are either eleven or twelve people in the family, but I'm not sure about that. The beauty of the whole thing is that these native People haven't allowed much of anything to encroach on how they live." Kalluk moved his hand as if to dispel a bad idea. "They're not unaware and they're far from stupid. They know what's going on in Alaska, if not in the world in general. Simply stated, they like their ways better—they like their lives better than what the new millennium can offer."

"They're a family, then? Blood relatives?" Tessa asked.

"In a sense, yes. Sons have brought wives and daughters husbands. But a few of the men and women aren't actual relatives." Kalluk's eyes showed some mirth—perhaps a bit of teasing. "Let me use an anthropological term: consanguinity."

Tessa smiled. "Yes, I know what that word means."

Kalluk smiled back at her. "The old Inuit concept of family isn't predicated on blood. A man or woman who joins a group is automatically family, and there's no distinction between them and the original blood members."

Jessie broke in. "I think Tessa would like to know how modern—or un-modern, if that's a word—these folks live, Kalluk. Right, Tessa?"

"Yes, I would. That's important to what I'm doing here."

Kalluk sat back in his chair. "Of course the People see jet contrails in the sky, and of course they talk to other folks who aren't following the traditional way of life. They've seen the pipeline, they've seen roads where there weren't even trails before. I suppose they know that cell phones and computers and things like that exist. But they don't *care*. That's where the beauty of it is. These people and others like them recognize and accept and love a sort of life that may never really touch us."

Jessie reached over and patted Kalluk affectionately on the shoulder. She said to Tessa, "My friend here is the type of guy who, if you ask him what time it is, will spend the rest of the day telling you how to build a clock. I'll tell you this, though: he's worth listening to, at least about the People." She considered a moment. "About hunting and native rights too." This time, she shoved the shoulder she'd just patted. "Don't go getting a swelled-up head, Kalluk."

Kalluk focused on Jessie for a long moment. His right hand reached across the table and grasped hers. "Will you marry me, Jessie?" he asked.

Jessie snorted. "Not on your life! I might just as well marry a rodeo cowboy. Do I look like I'm crazy?"

"I guess that means no," Kalluk said with mock heartbreak in his voice.

"How long have you two known one another?" Tessa asked, laughing.

"Forever," Jessie said.

"Not nearly long enough," Kalluk said. "But her attitude could give us problems in the future. Maybe she'll—"

"Maybe she has things to do beyond listening to your nonsense," Jessie said. "Come on, I'll take you to the cabin and have someone drop off the old Jeep later. You need anything from the store here?"

"No, I don't think so." Kalluk stood up. "Look, this is all clear to me. We're all going out, no? Jessie will whine and carry on a bit, but she'll go. R. E.'s tongue has been hanging out since I first mentioned the whole deal. The only way to leave him behind would be to hog-tie him to the foundation of his mercantile. And Tessa . . . well, her eyes said yes as soon as we met. Maybe she'd have to be hog-tied too, to leave her behind. So, unless I'm wrong, we're set."

He grinned and turned away. Jessie stood, drank the last of her coffee, and waved as she hustled after Kalluk.

R. E. and Tessa remained at the table. "What do you think?" he asked.

"About the field trip? About Kalluk?"

"Both."

"I've got to admit that now that I know Jessie is going,

79

it's more enticing to me. If she's a guide, she must know her stuff. I like her. The trip could be the high point of my time in Alaska, at least from the university's perspective."

"And about Kalluk?"

"Well, it's hard to say, since I just met the man twenty minutes ago." She mused for a few moments. "He seems rather taken with himself, but that's probably not strange for someone who's in the spotlight as much as he is. I'm sure he's nice enough."

"Well. More coffee?" R. E. asked, standing.

"No thanks. I've got work waiting for me." She got up from the table.

"Think about the trip, OK? And about Kalluk: he's kinda like Fuzz. He grows on you."

"Maybe he does," Tessa said.

———◆═◆◆═◆———

That evening, just after dark, Tessa went to her kitchen at the sound of a vehicle coming up her driveway. The headlights were askew—one pointed down a few feet in front of the vehicle and the other seemed to be searching the depths of the sky. The driver wasn't showing the car any mercy—it pounded and swayed its way over potholes and ruts at twice the speed Tessa used on the same stretch of driveway. Tessa clicked on the outside light. The vehicle, she saw, was an old WWII Jeep. Although manufactured with no enclosure around the cab, this one had an obviously homemade wooden boxlike affair to spare the driver from the elements. The Jeep pulled in front first and then backed around to face the driveway. Tessa noticed that there was no license plate at either end and that one of the brake lights was out. She watched as Kalluk stepped out of the driver's side and R. E. and Jessie from the passenger side.

Tessa tugged open her door as the trio stepped up to it. "Come on in," she said. "I'll put coffee on."

"Don't bother with coffee, Tessa," Jessie said. "This is an official visit—not a coffee and chat one."

"Official? I don't get it," Tessa said.

The cabin suddenly seemed very small with three extra people in it. A little confused, Tessa said, "Official or not, let's sit down. Come on."

R. E., Kalluk, and Jessie took the couch, sitting elbow to elbow, their coats still on and buttoned. The three of them looked vaguely uncomfortable, like Tessa's students did when they attempted to explain why their term papers were late. Tessa pulled the chair from her worktable around to face them. "What's up?" she asked.

Jessie answered. "We're here to tell you more about the trip and to answer questions. We've discussed this, and we'd really like to have you come along. We think you'd bring a lot if you joined us."

Tessa was about to speak when Kalluk took the floor. "For one thing," he said, "it'd be good for the credibility of the entire idea—having a university anthropologist a part of the group when we meet with the natives. What you observe and write about would generate some academic and general interest in what we find." He smiled. "And it'd bring in even more people when I speak at schools too."

R. E. was next. "I want you to really see Alaska, Tess. I want you to love it as much as I do. Long after the trip, no matter where you are, what you tell people will have a real effect on how they perceive us and our land, and I think that's important."

Jessie nodded. "There's this too: can you imagine being out in the wilderness for a couple weeks or more without another woman to talk to? I've done it a few times in my business, and it's the same each time. Guys jabber like excited kids for the first couple of days, and after that it's pretty much grunts and groans and complaining about the food and discussions about whether Ford or Chevrolet engines are better." Her grin spread into a full smile. "Seriously—I'd love to have you along, and I really do think you'd be a great addition. Will you think about it?"

Tessa felt frozen to the spot, not sure of what to say.

"You must have questions. Ask away, Tessa," Kalluk said.

"I have—but first I need to say that this is a surprise and quite a compliment, and I appreciate it. I'm just a little overwhelmed, I guess."

"Maybe if we can give you some answers you'll be less overwhelmed," R. E. pointed out.

"Maybe so." Tessa thought for a moment. "OK—how many people are involved?"

"No more than six if you join up," Kalluk said. "The four of us and a pair of Inuit brothers I know. Any more and we'd be like a safari, and any fewer we might be undermanned if we hit weather."

"That's a big 'if' too," Jessie said. "This isn't the best time of the year for this."

"No," Kalluk agreed. "Probably not. But this is when we'll be able to meet up with the people I want to be with—and the ones Tessa wants to study."

"There'll be four sleds for the first part of the trek," R. E. said.

Tessa looked at him questioningly.

"Snowmobiles, Tess. We're borrowing them from Jessie's guiding operation. We fill the tanks before we set out and ride them until they're half empty. Then we mark the spot and go ahead on foot, hauling our tents and provisions on runners and on our backs."

"How far out will the trip go?" Tessa asked.

"Maybe a hundred and twenty miles," Jessie said. "But it's not the number of miles but the kind of terrain we'll be covering—and the weather."

Kalluk nodded. "There's some rough ground between here and where we're headed. Nothing anywhere near impassible, but it won't be a Sunday jaunt, either."

"What about food, medical supplies, communications equipment—all that?"

"Covered," Kalluk said. "We'll be hauling MREs—meals ready to eat. They're lightweight, nourishing, easy to heat. Some of them don't taste half bad, either. We'll bring standard medical emergency supplies."

"Communications will be a little tough out there," Jessie admitted. "Cell phones of course won't work, and radio contact isn't really effective. The only units we could get are heavy and expensive and not too reliable. But I've taken dozens of trips out supplied just as we'll be, and I've had no problems that radio contact would have solved."

"That's a major point, Tess," R. E. said. "Jessie does this sort of thing for a living, and Kalluk has been out many times alone or with groups. They know what they're doing."

The conversation went on for another ten minutes, touching on weather, required supplies, anticipated distance traveled per day, as well as the minutia of any such undertaking. After a few moments of silence, the trio stood from the couch.

"We'll leave you alone now," Jessie said. The men murmured agreement. At the door, R. E. said, "Think about it, Tess. Call me when you've decided, no matter when it is."

"I will," Tessa said. Each of the visitors then shook hands with Tessa rather formally, almost as if they were investors considering a joint business venture. Tessa watched from her kitchen window as the single red taillight of the old Jeep disappeared around the curve in the driveway. She stood for a minute looking out into the darkness and then went back into the living room. She checked the fire; it didn't need wood and was pushing out heat nicely. She sat on the couch where Kalluk had been and reviewed the conversation.

She remembered a conversation she'd had with her father when she was thirteen and considering going on a two-week trip to a summer art and crafts camp. "There are some things that can have the life and fun analyzed right out of them, honey," her dad had said. "Think things over, pray about them, talk with me or your mom or your friends, and then make your decision. OK?" He'd smiled then and hugged her tightly. "'Course, if you did go, you'd have to be very, very careful or you might just have a great time—and you might even learn something."

The camp had been wonderful, and Tessa made two good friends, both of whom she continued to communicate with through letters and telephone calls.

OK, so I'm a little . . . cautious by nature. Contemplative, maybe. Solidly analytical. I like to turn things over in my mind, see all the facets. I'm a college professor, after all. I'm supposed to question and inquire, right?

Tessa pushed up from her slouch on the sofa and started to the kitchen. Halfway there she made a U-turn and ended up once again sprawled on the couch.

There's not a thing in the world wrong with being cautious. It's not that I'm afraid to go out into Alaska, not at all. It's just that . . . what? What is it? She sighed. *It's just that I'm a bookish geek who acts ninety-five instead of thirty-six . . .*

"I'm in," she said aloud. "I'm in."

6

Jessie, Tessa soon learned from R. E. and others, was an enigma in the Alaskan wilderness guide business. Although her clients got to take all the shots they wanted—in or out of season and in any number they cared to—she never hauled out trophy heads or bloody bear pelts or hundreds of pounds of freshly killed game meat. In fact, her treks never brought about the death of a single animal.

Jessie's customers at Alaskan Ventures shot Nikons and Canons and Minoltas—no firearms except the rifle Jessie packed for emergencies were allowed.

She'd started Alaskan Ventures almost fifteen years ago after apprenticing for a good part of her life with her father, a hunting and fishing guide. Jessie's business had struggled along for four years, barely covering expenses, until a young photographer on assignment from *National Geographic* signed on for a long trek. The subsequent photo essay, which got the cover and nine full pages inside the ultra-prestigious magazine, mentioned Jessie's name and that of her guiding operation several times in the text. Even now, ten years after the magazine appeared, she was forced to turn away business for each of the forays she announced.

With Jessie orchestrating the gathering of supplies, the groundwork for the trip came together quickly and efficiently. Four beat-up but dependable snowmobiles appeared behind R. E.'s store one morning, along with three tightly packed two-person tents. Cases of meals-ready-to-eat were stacked on two tow-along carriers on runners. The tents, patched but secure, were from Jessie's company provisions. Nevertheless, she unfolded each and checked it for even the smallest tears. A howling sixty-mile-per-hour wind, she pointed out, could turn a quarter-inch rip into a gaping hole in less than seconds.

The army surplus Jeep Kalluk was using for the duration became a familiar sight around Fairview and in the mercantile lot. Tessa, accustomed to the almost total silence of her cabin site, was frequently shaken from sound sleep by the tractor-like roar of the Jeep as Kalluk left and returned to his cabin. Tessa hadn't known the ramshackle little shelter even existed before Kalluk arrived, and was surprised to find that it was considerably less than a mile from her home, just beyond a long, sloping, heavily treed berm she'd not yet explored.

Kalluk warned Tessa not to be concerned about the wolf tracks she'd be finding in the snow around her cabin. Fuzz was a far-ranging creature by instinct, and he'd soon find and explore her living area. Kalluk was right. Tessa soon no longer shivered when she saw the paw marks in the snow.

One day, however, Tessa found a bloody mess—tufts of deep brown fur and chunks of flesh—near her trash can. The tracks told the story. Fuzz had eliminated her raccoon problem. She sniffed and, standing beside her cabin in an intermittent cold wind, rubbed the back of her mitten across her eyes. Quick mental pictures of the raccoons peering out of her trash can at her, their eyes wide, more curious than anything else, brought a lump to her throat. *They were a pain in the neck, but they were harmless enough, and so . . . cute. That dog—or wolf, or whatever he is—isn't domesticated.* She started toward her Jeep and then stopped. *Maybe Kalluk isn't completely domesticated, either. The guy is handsome in the same way Fuzz is handsome, in a semi-frightening way, as if he doesn't really belong in the type of life most of us know. Maybe that's why R. E. is so fascinated with Kalluk.* She tugged the Jeep's door open and slid behind the wheel. *Maybe that's why I'm a little fascinated with Kalluk too,* she admitted to herself.

Meeloa was quiet for a long moment after Tessa told her about the raccoon incident on their way to call on the elders. "You shouldn't be surprised," she finally said.

"It's not really a matter of being surprised. Back home, dogs kill woodchucks and skunks and raccoons. It's . . . well, the way Fuzz slides around, so secretive and sneaky. And when he killed the raccoons I was asleep, not ten feet away, and I didn't hear a thing. Nothing. And from the amount of fur and blood, he must have killed at least two of them—maybe three or four."

"Wolves don't kill like dogs, Tess. They'll bay and yelp as they're running something down, but the actual kill is silent. It's like they don't need to prove anything by growling and snarling. And they kill for food, not because another animal is strange to them. If Fuzz's tummy was full, he wouldn't have given your raccoons a second glance."

"Kalluk doesn't feed him?" Tessa asked, incredulously.

"Yeah, but not much. Maybe kibble once a day, but Fuzz has several hundreds of thousands of acres to scrounge up a meal in. It's only natural that Kalluk would let him provide most of his own food." She smiled. "Anyway, can you imagine Kalluk opening a can of Mighty Dog?" After a moment, she added, "It's Fuzz's instincts at work. There's a lot more wolf than dog in most of those crossbreeds."

Tessa nodded. "I still have a lot to learn about Alaska," she said.

Meeloa smiled warmly at her friend. "So have I," she said.

Tessa took the turn off the road, stopped, shifted into four-wheel drive, and plowed through the low drifts that had accumulated since their last visit to the elders a week ago. Snow had been light thus far into the winter. Christmas was barely two weeks away, and there'd not been a single storm.

"You'll tell them today we won't be around to visit for a few weeks?" Tessa said as she and Meeloa trudged to the cabin door from the Jeep.

"I'm afraid they won't like it much—you going out there—but I'll tell them."

Tessa didn't respond. Meeloa had made it clear that she wasn't in favor of the field trip, either. "Jessie rarely takes her photo trips out this time of year. It's crazy, Tess."

Explaining that the meet-up with the People wouldn't be possible later in the year didn't sway Meeloa's opinion. They'd both decided not talking about the trip was better than arguing about it.

Now they sat in the straight-backed chairs with mugs of steaming zibalsl clutched in their hands, its library-paste texture holding the beverage thickly in place even when the mugs moved in conversational gestures. When Meeloa explained about Tessa's upcoming trek, the elders didn't seem at all happy about it. Meeloa translated as well as she was able, but all four of the elders were speaking over one another, each increasing volume to be heard, and each responding to the increased volume with yet more volume and arm waving. As Tessa watched the melee, she felt acutely uncomfortable and very sorry that she'd caused these fine old people such strife. Their eyes, even in the heat of argument with Meeloa, showed that they were concerned about Tessa. One phrase her friend translated as the furor wound down brought a lump to Tessa's throat: "Tessa is a good and fine woman who is in our hearts. But she does not have our blood."

The meeting ended rather quickly. As Tessa left, each of the Inuits, though not physically demonstrative by nature, embraced her as if she were a beloved daughter.

"Their eyes were sad," Tessa said as she started her Jeep's engine and shifted into first gear.

"Yeah. They—the People—believe that they're the only ones who know Alaska, that only they have the blood of the land in their veins." After a moment, she said, "They care about you."

"Jessie will be shooting pictures. I'll bring photos to them afterward."

Meeloa smiled. "All you need to do is bring *you* back to them, Tess. The pictures will be window dressing."

Tessa drove mechanically to Meeloa's cabin. There was little further conversation. As Meeloa was leaving the Jeep, she stopped with the door open and reached over to touch Tessa's shoulder. "Take care, girl," she said. "If I don't see you before you guys leave, have a good, safe trip."

Tessa covered Meeloa's hand with her own. "Thanks. We'll take the pictures to the elders as soon as I get back, OK?"

"I'll look forward to it," Meeloa said; then she smiled and closed the door.

Tessa was perplexed as she drove off. *I don't understand this. It's not a moon landing or a dive to the deepest part of the sea. It's only a field trip. Where could I be safer than with two—possibly four, if those brothers show up as they're supposed to—native Alaskans, one of whom guides trips like this for a living? The elders were all upset, as if I were never coming back. Even Meeloa, who knows all the people involved, and knows their skills, is worried. Her eyes showed that.* The low-volume blather on the radio was suddenly acutely irritating. Tess snapped off the radio, noticed that the light snow that'd been falling most of the day had become heavier, and reluctantly turned the radio back on. *See?* she told herself. *Just like a native Alaskan—always listening for weather bulletins.*

She had plenty to do at home: a final review of her list, reporting for her department at the university to catch up on, files to edit—and some dinner and breakfast dishes that'd somehow taken up permanent residence in her sink. Nevertheless, she turned into R. E.'s parking lot. Kalluk's Jeep, she noticed, wasn't there in the spot where he usually parked it, and she felt a tiny twang of disappointment. She sat behind her wheel for a moment, slightly confused. *What's this all about? What difference does it make if Kalluk's here or not? I'm coming to see R. E.*

The mix of aromas from within the mercantile greeted her as they always did. The coffee smelled especially rich today. R. E. was in the front of the store, smiling at her.

"Hey, Tess. I was watching you through the window. I thought you'd fallen asleep out there."

"Lost in space for a minute," she said. "What kind of a deal can I get on a cup of coffee and a cookie?"

"Grab a table in back, and I'll see what I can do. No cookies today, though—I've got actual doughnuts!"

"No! Go away—you have not. You're teasing me."

"Just you wait an' see." R. E. walked to the counter, where a large aluminum bowl rested near the cash register. Tessa hung her coat over the back of a chair and sat at a table to the rear of the little snack area. In a moment R. E.—with a smile a yard wide—strode over to her, two mugs of coffee in one hand and a pair of large and slightly misshapen doughnuts on a paper plate in the other. "The same lady who bakes the cookies took a try at these little sweethearts," he said.

"I haven't had a doughnut—except for those plastic-wrapped lumps—since I got here. Those are beautiful, R. E."

"You betcha. Shall we have at them?"

Tessa didn't answer as she reached toward the plate. She closed her eyes with her first bite and sighed with pleasure. When they finished, the only remaining evidence of the two doughnuts was a few almost microscopic crumbs on the paper plate. They sighed in unison and sipped at their coffee.

"Six more days and we're outta here, Tess," R. E. said. "A friend of Kalluk's brought a message from the people we're meeting."

"Great! I'm ready right now." She thought for a moment. "Christmas in the wilds of Alaska, then."

"Yeah. It'll be fun."

"It will. You know, I don't think I'm supposed to be so excited about what's allegedly kind of an academic exercise for my university. But I sure am."

R. E. grinned across the table. "I'm glad you're excited. And guess what? So am I."

Kalluk's voice startled both of them. Neither had heard him come in from the back door and storage area of the mercantile, where the provisions for the trip were being cached.

Kalluk nodded to them. "I just pulled in to check the MREs—I want to do a count to make sure we got all the meals we paid for. Am I disturbing something?"

"Not at all," R. E. said. "Grab a cup of coffee, sit down with us. There's doughnuts up front. Help yourself."

"Can't. I need to see Jessie and make a couple of telephone calls. Besides, you two looked like you were deep in a conversation. Anyway—see you later." He ducked back into the storeroom and pulled the door closed behind him.

Tessa cleared her throat and redirected the conversation. "I'm sure I have everything I'm supposed to have. I've gone over my list a gazillion times, and if I'm missing something, I can't imagine what it could be."

"I'm all set too." He laughed. "I haven't been this wound up about anything since I quit my stocks and bonds job—and that's really saying something."

Two native women came through the front door, one of them clutching the hand of a little boy. They went to the material counter, and R. E. left the table when one of the ladies motioned him over. He grabbed up a sucker from the candy display for the boy on his way.

Tessa watched R. E. as he waited on his customers. She could hear sounds and an occasional laugh but couldn't hear clearly enough to follow the conversation. The words didn't really matter: the smiles and tones of voice conveyed the fact that the women—and the boy—knew and trusted R. E. and that he liked and respected them. *It'd be wonderful if everyone could find a way to be happy in life, just as R. E. has. I can't say I understand his life here or why it's so fulfilling to him. I wonder if it's because R. E. is basically an uncomplicated guy, one who knows how to meet his own needs, knows what he has to do to keep himself happy? He's a good man,* she decided, *and a rare one.*

"So," R. E. said as he sat back down across the table from Tessa. "You looked like you were lost in space again."

"Maybe. I was thinking about the trip."

"Hard not to, isn't—"

R. E. was interrupted as the mercantile door slammed open with enough force to rebound off the stop and make the glass rattle. Two men—obviously native Alaskans—dressed in silver-gray fur coats that reached to the top of their tall, laced boots, stepped into the store and stood side by side a foot apart, looking like a pair of perfectly matched bookends. Each fellow was relatively short, about five foot five, and each appeared to be almost as wide as he was tall. Their skin was a honey-ochre color, and their eyes were black pebbles set into deep folds. Their hair, black and abundant, hung rather limply over their shoulders and to their chests.

The silence in the store went on forever. R. E. stood.

"Albin," said one man. "Randall," said the other.

95

R. E. stood there in confusion for a moment. "Uh, what can I do for you fellas?"

"Kalluk," Randall said.

Tessa and R. E. made the connection immediately. Tessa shoved back her chair and followed R. E. as he rushed to the brothers. He shook hands with both of them and introduced himself and Tessa.

"I'm glad to meet you Albin, Randall," Tessa said. "Kalluk speaks well of you. I'm going on the trek too."

"Kalluk's not here right now, but I'll be glad to drive you over to his cabin," R. E. said. Tessa noticed that R. E. was speaking much louder than he would normally—the unfortunate reaction of many people to someone they don't think has a complete grasp of English. "Or, how about some coffee here? I don't serve regular food, but I have snacks."

The brothers looked at one another as if conferring telepathically. "Go to Kalluk now," Randall said. "Coffee another time."

"Fine, fine," R. E. said, again too loud. He turned to Tessa. "You want to stay here, Tess? I'll only be a few minutes. Or, I can lock up. It doesn't matter."

"No, I'm going to head home. I've got some papers to shove around." She nodded at the Inuits. "See you soon," she said. In a much lower voice, barely above a whisper, she said, "Quit hollering at those two. They seem to understand English just fine."

❖

In her Jeep, Tessa keyed the engine to life and let it idle for a time. *Now* those *guys* *look like native Alaskans—what people used to call Eskimos. And those coats. Unless I miss my guess, they were made from wolf hides.*

Although it was barely a few minutes after midafternoon, the meager light of day was already receding into the darkness. Tessa considered flicking on her headlights and decided it was a bit early for them. Doing so would have been very lower 48. She pulled into her usual parking place adjacent to the cabin and stepped out into the cold. The Jeep's heater had, in the few minutes the engine had been running, heated up nicely. The outdoor chill brought her a quick shiver as she walked to her front door, and she looked forward to adding a couple of logs and stoking up the fire in her woodstove.

She stopped a few yards from the cabin. The front door was wide open, and it was hanging precariously from a single hinge. Even in the murky light Tessa could see slashes in the wood, as if the door had been struck several times with an axe or large knife. There was no sound from inside, no indication that anyone was still in there. Snow had blown into the cabin through the open door, and a fluffy line a couple of inches high had formed along the base of the door. Tessa realized that the invasion had happened a while ago—an hour, perhaps a couple of hours. A heavy, barnyard-type odor reached her—the reek of manure and rot. There was a thud from inside the cabin, followed by the screech of collapsing, breaking wood. At first it all seemed otherworldly; the facts didn't really register. Just beyond the door, where the heat from inside had partially melted the snow, her eyes found a paw mark exactly like the ones she'd seen in the woods scribed into the slush. Another tremor shook her body. This time it wasn't from the cold—it was from raw, unthinking fear that was rapidly becoming panic. Her instinct—her human fight or flight predisposition—demanded that she run.

Tessa did just that.

She jammed her key into the Jeep's ignition, cranked the engine, floored the gas pedal, and popped the clutch. The knobby tires screamed as they tried to bite into the hard-frozen ground, and the acrid blue smoke of burning rubber rolled from the wheel wells. In the past few minutes the darkness had thickened. Tessa fumbled with the light switch not for concerns of safety but simply because she couldn't see and was driving like a lunatic down the tree-shrouded little access road from the cabin to the highway.

The Jeep skidded out onto the asphalt almost sideways, engine howling. The halogen lights of an approaching vehicle dipped toward the pavement sharply as the driver jammed on his brakes. Tessa fought the steering wheel as the other vehicle slewed past her. For the briefest part of a heartbeat the face of one of the Inuit brothers in the right-hand seat of R. E.'s truck strobed past her. Even in that minuscule bit of time the fact registered in her mind that the man's face showed no more surprise or fear than if he were watching a dull television program on a sleepy evening.

For a moment there was silence, and then R. E. was dragging her Jeep's door open, calling, "Tessa! Tessa!" His face was white with fear. Her engine had stalled at the end of her skid, but Tessa still gripped the steering wheel with all her strength.

"There's a bear in my cabin," she managed to get out. R. E. leaned into the Jeep, and over his shoulder she saw the brothers. They stood a few feet behind R. E., side by side as when they had entered the store, their faces showing nothing. Both of their coats were open at the front now, and each held a massive pistol, muzzle upward. Tessa had once seen a Clint Eastwood Dirty Harry film; this was the same weapon the fictional rogue cop carried, and scenes of the violence that were the major parts of the film flashed in her mind.

"Where . . ." Albin began when another vehicle, its engine as loud as that of a NASCAR winner, skidded to a stop. Before the army Jeep was completely halted, Kalluk was out of it on the driver's side and Fuzz on the passenger's. Albin and Randall, guns now holstered, met Kalluk. A few words were said, and the three of them and the wolf-dog piled into Kalluk's vehicle. The engine bellowed as Kalluk blasted onto the access road to the cabin.

Tessa cranked her stalled engine. R. E., still leaning inside the vehicle, reached for her hand at the ignition switch to stop her. "No—we'll go back to the store in my truck, Tess. Your Jeep is OK here. Come on . . ."

"No!" Tessa snapped, louder than she intended to. "I'm going to my cabin." R. E. began to speak, looked into her eyes, and quickly thought better of it. He slammed the driver's door, raced around the front of the Jeep, and piled into the passenger seat. Before he could close his door the Jeep was in motion as Tessa stomped on the gas pedal.

I should have stayed in my Jeep, laid on the horn, and scared the bear out into the woods—just like R. E. and Meeloa told me to handle something like that. But no, instead I have to pull my poor, defenseless girly act right in front of the men I'm supposed to go out into the wild with—men who need to depend on me out there just like I'll depend on them.

Tessa flinched as R. E. gently touched her shoulder.

99

"Sorry," he said. "I thought maybe you'd want to talk a little. Kind of calm down. You've had quite a scare."

Her reply was more than childish, and she knew that as soon as she said it. "I wasn't scared."

"OK," R. E. said. "Fine with me, Tess. I'd have been scared stiff. At least you had the sense to . . . to do something."

"Do something? I ran in a panic, is what I did. That's not doing something." Tessa cringed at the heat and sharpness of her own words. "I feel like a woman from a cheap romance novel, running to the big, powerful, macho men for help. What are those brothers and Kalluk and you going to think of me?"

"Tessa," R. E. said gently. "Come on. It was a bear, and it was in your home. You'd have to be nuts to do anything other than what you did. Do you think those guys expected you to wrestle the bear to the ground and beat it into submission with your fists?"

"Well . . . no, I guess not." She forced a smile, shifted into first gear, and clattered off the shoulder, onto the road, and back into her driveway. They skidded around the last curve before the cabin, and Tessa hit the brakes. The tableau in front of them looked like a bigger-than-life illustration from a tourist poster—the bear, massive, on its back feet, a head taller than a tall man, was pinned in the beam of Kalluk's halogen torch. The brothers were twenty feet apart, their pistols extended in the two-handed grip, the red dots of laser sights like dime-sized rubies on the matted brownish-black fur. Kalluk, at the apex of a triangle formed by the three men, was a dozen feet in front of the brothers, and his wolf-dog was lunging at the heavy chain around his neck.

The bear, whose impossibly long fangs were glinting in the

harsh light, seemed to waver on his feet as if momentarily losing his balance. His warning to the men and the wolf was a deep, throaty roar that rose in pitch steadily and then stopped abruptly to begin again. A long string of spittle hung from the bear's lower jaw, looking bizarrely like a sparkling jeweled pendant in the piercing illumination.

Fuzz's challenge was lower, a hard rumble, a sound that remained steady as he strained against the chain. Kalluk hauled him off his front feet and shouted a single word in Inuit. Fuzz took a half step back, still in front of Kalluk, his eyes never leaving the bear.

The bear swayed again as if dizzy and took a shuffling step toward Kalluk. Both the brothers thumbed back the hammers on their pistols, and the metallic clicking sound somehow penetrated the growling and snarling. Tessa and R. E. had moved from her Jeep to a few feet behind the triangle.

"No! Don't shoot him," Tessa screamed, but her voice was swallowed by a shouted barrage of Inuit from Kalluk. Albin and Randall eased the hammers back into a safety position, but the red laser sight dots still held on the bear's chest.

The huge animal attempted another step forward, stumbled, fought for his balance, and then crashed down onto his front feet. As his jaw struck the frozen ground, his teeth made a distinct snapping sound. Now on four feet, he backed away a couple of steps, snarled at Fuzz and at the men, and made a clumsy turn. As he lumbered off toward the woods, weaving, his entire body listed to one side or the other as he plowed through the snow. Once out of the light the bear disappeared in the darkness.

Kalluk crouched for a moment, slipped the chain over

Fuzz's head, said a single word in his native language, and then stood and looked off at the woods. Then he turned and walked toward Tessa and R. E. The brothers intercepted him, and the three men talked briefly. Tessa saw Kalluk nod and smile before he again started toward her and R. E. Fuzz was a half stride behind his master, in the heel position, seeming to glide behind the man.

"He was a big one," Kalluk said. "Had some age on him too. Did you see the gray around his muzzle? Teeth still looked good, though."

Tessa found her voice. "Thanks for not letting them shoot him, Kalluk."

"There was no reason to kill that ol' boy," Kalluk said. "He wasn't an immediate danger—unless we got too close to him. He was half asleep. You saw how clumsy he was, how he moved like he'd gotten into a patch of fermented berries. Something disturbed him in his winter den, broke his hibernation."

"What would do that?" R. E. asked.

"If he dug his own den—and lots of them do—it could have caved in on him. Or, wolves could have found him. He wasn't cut up, though, so it probably wasn't wolves. He's big enough to fight off a few of them in a tight area, but he'd have some damage if that's what happened. I don't know. He blundered onto the cabin, and his instinct took him inside, looking for food." He grinned at Tessa. "And here we are." Kalluk stepped into the small space between Tessa and R. E. "Let's take a look inside—see how much trouble the ol' rascal caused."

Albin and Randall stood next to Tessa's Jeep and watched the others, apparently not interested in whatever damage the inside of the cabin had suffered. They'd seen it many times before, their casual posture stated, and it was nothing new.

Kalluk touched the splintered wood of the doorjamb. "Nice stout door," he commented. "We can move the hinge up a couple of inches, and it'll work fine. Won't take a minute." He turned to Tessa. "You have basic tools—hammer, screwdrivers, stuff like that?"

"Sure." She eased past Kalluk into the cabin and clicked on the overhead light. Her gasp was involuntary.

"Hey, it's not so bad," Kalluk assured her.

"Looks worse than it is," R. E. offered.

Tessa's upended work table and the snowstorm of sticky notes, loose-leaf pages, and scattered floppies was the centerpiece of the mess. The dozens of journals and reference books that littered the floor with their pages fluttering in the breeze looked like a flock of gravely wounded birds. Something crackled under Tessa and Kalluk's boots as they stepped closer to the frenzy of paper.

"Corn flakes," R. E. said from behind them. He pointed to the box, which was split from top to bottom as if with a sharp cleaver, on the floor against the couch. Several cassettes were strewn about, and a couple appeared to have been crushed or chewed, with lengths of tape protruding in twisted loops. They moved to the kitchen, walking slowly, as if any further sound would make things worse.

A cabinet door had been torn off and cast aside. A can of tomato soup rested on the counter, draining red liquid from a series of punctures that formed a neat *U* on the container's surface. There was a light sifting of flour on the floor, and the Pillsbury sack, ripped to shreds, had somehow ended

103

up on top of the refrigerator. An unopened jar of grape jelly stood neatly, almost precisely, in the center of the otherwise empty sink. The Mr. Coffee was on its side, the carafe a foot from the base. Bits and larger shards of glass sparkled on the floor and along the counter—Tessa's juice glass and coffee mug that she'd left on the drainer after rinsing them that morning.

"Could have been a whole lot worse," Kalluk said. "You must have gotten here before he could do a real hungry-bear-type search. Then the rest of us showed up. If we hadn't, you can bet he'd have gotten into the other cabinets and maybe the refrigerator too." He looked over the damage. "Umm . . . your coffeemaker looks OK unless the pot is cracked." Kalluk took a pair of steps, picked up the carafe, and inspected it carefully. "Nope, it's fine."

"Are you asking me to make coffee?" Tessa asked incredulously. "My home has been savaged, and you want coffee?"

"Well . . . sure. Like I said, you got off easy. We can straighten all this up in ten minutes, while the coffee perks or drips or whatever it does in a Mr. Coffee. All you lost was some flour and a box of corn flakes, right?"

"That mass of paper out there represents months of study and writing," Tessa said. "Look at those cassettes—they're ruined."

"I'll make coffee," R. E. said. "I know where everything is. Tess, why don't you see if you can put some order to the papers?"

Tessa mumbled, "Thanks, R .E.," and crunched her way over to her work area. She could hear most of their conversation as she crouched on the floor, shuffling papers.

"She seems upset," Kalluk observed, as if he were commenting on the weather.

"Well, yeah, a bear invaded her cabin. Anybody'd be upset. Wouldn't you?"

"Nah—what good would it do? A bear is a bear. It's not like he chose her for a vendetta or something. This was the place he ended up at as he was wandering around."

"Maybe Tess is worried he'll break in again when she's here."

"Won't happen, R. E."

"No? Why won't it?"

"'Cause I'm leaving Fuzz here to watch the place. He's no match for the bear in a close fight, but he's fast enough and bright enough to keep him away from the cabin."

R. E. didn't have an answer. The conversation of the two men was replaced by the clinking of cups and the drawing of water from the sink faucet. When they moved to the coffee machine at the end of the kitchen, she could no longer distinguish their words. She crawled through the mess, closing and stacking books and journals in her arms. She set those aside and muscled her table to its feet. It was no more shaky than it had been pre-bear, but its surface at one end bore a series of deep scratches about four inches long. She shuddered as she touched them and crouched again, gathering index cards. *Maybe Kalluk was right,* she admitted to herself. *This isn't nearly as bad as it looked at first. It'll take some time to get my cards and notes in order, and I'll need to do some sweeping, is all.*

She set the stack of index cards on the table and began collecting the cassette tapes. Two were definitely ruined and another two were damaged, but the actual tape appeared intact. The cassettes contained her own comments and observations; she breathed more easily when she found her box of microcassettes under several pages of handwritten notes, still secure in the plastic storage case in which she'd kept them. Those contained her interviews with the elders, the throat singing, and conversations with various native Inuits she'd been able to talk to and record.

Tessa looked up as Kalluk came into the room, a cup of coffee in each hand. "Everything OK?" he asked. He handed her coffee to her.

"It's not all that bad—not like I first thought," Tessa said.

"Good," Kalluk said. "I didn't mean to be smart earlier when I said there wasn't much damage. It's just that I've seen stuff like this before. You really did get off easy, Tess."

"I know that now. It was just shocking to see my place like this."

Kalluk took a long sip of coffee. "Maybe I spoke without thinking. For what it's worth, I don't blame you for being afraid of that bear. I respect what you're doing here and your interest in going on this trip. It's not going to be a vacation and you know that, yet you're still ready to go. That says a lot about you. So does the fact that R. E.'s told me you genuinely care about native Alaskans—that we're not little bits of an academic collection of cultures to you."

His eyes were again on hers. She couldn't be certain whether they were a deep chestnut or a penetrating black. Either way, there was an intensity to them that was a bit frightening, as if holding his gaze would draw her into some sort of bottomless abyss. She wanted to look away—and didn't want to.

"That's kind of you to say, Kalluk," she managed. It took her a second to form another thought. "I know I have a great deal to learn about Alaska, but I do know I love it here."

The grinding of corn flakes under R. E.'s boots announced his return from the kitchen. He looked quizzically from Tessa to Kalluk and then back to Tessa. "What's up?" he asked.

"I just complimented Tessa on her courage for being willing to be a part of our little expedition. I'm really impressed by that."

"She's an impressive lady," R. E. said and glanced at Tessa. She felt herself blush. He looked through the hanging front door. "I've got enough coffee for Albin and Randall, Kalluk. Call them in, OK?"

"I would, but neither one of them is housebroken."

Tessa and R. E. gawked at him.

"Come on," he said with a grin. "That was a joke. Those guys are every bit as civilized as . . ."

"As Fuzz," R. E. supplied.

"Right." Kalluk laughed. "But I'll bring them in. I've got to spend some time with them about the trip."

"Oh?" R. E. asked.

"Yeah. Randall gave me a bit of news a few minutes ago, just before Tessa skidded out onto the road. He and Albin brought a message from the group I'm looking to connect with. To catch them as we planned to, we need to set out the day after tomorrow."

7

The roar of the ancient Jeep carrying Kalluk, Albin, and Randall had barely faded before Tessa and R. E. were hard at work putting Tessa's home back together.

"There. That ought to do it," R. E. said, stepping back from his job. He eased the door shut, checking the clearance between the door itself and the step plate at the bottom and door frame at the top and sides. Everything came together smoothly and the knob/lock mechanism joined with a comforting click.

Tessa, sweeping the last of the corn flakes into a dustpan, smiled across the room. "Thanks, R. E." She dumped the contents of the dustpan into the trash and leaned the broom against the wall. "Let's sit for a minute," she said. As she passed the window she caught the gray blur of Fuzz's coat against the snow as he drifted by. "There goes Fuzz again. I wonder if he's going to trot around the cabin all night long."

"I doubt it. He'll probably find a place out of the wind to rest and make his rounds every so often. I doubt that a field mouse could get within fifty yards of the cabin without him knowing it and doing something about it."

They sat on the couch, and both sank back gratefully and a little wearily.

"Long day," R. E. observed.

"Mmmm," Tessa agreed. "It's hard to believe that everything's come together after all the planning and talking and provisioning. But it's true—we'll crank up those snowmobiles day after tomorrow."

"Any second thoughts?"

Tessa didn't reply for a moment. "I was thinking about that as I was sweeping," she said. "No—no second thoughts. I'll admit to a swarm of bumblebees in my stomach since Kalluk told us, though."

R. E. chuckled. "Me too. But, how many people do you know who've been able to pursue an adventure like this one in the course of their lives? I know that to Jessie and Kalluk and the brothers it's probably no big deal. But to me—and you—wow!"

"You've already experienced a real adventure, R. E. I'd say changing your whole life is a heck of an adventure."

"Me? Come on, Tess. I'm a storekeeper."

"But you were once a stocks and bonds man with a ton of money and all the toys in the world, and you dumped it all and came here with no idea if the whole thing was going to work for you, or if you'd end up pumping gas on the midnight shift for minimum wage in Fairbanks."

"It wasn't quite that bad."

"Oh, hush. If I want to make a hero out of you, I will."

"That's fine with me."

They sat together a few minutes in an easy silence, the

night soundless outside, the warmth of the woodstove making them almost comfortable enough to doze off.

"I'm kind of wondering how you'll get on with Kalluk on the trip. He can be kind of . . . well . . . abrasive."

The question pulled Tessa back to full consciousness. She considered for a moment before she spoke. "I suppose he could be a bit hard to take at times. But I respect what he's doing with his life and the fact that he's lived in the wilds with the People as an equal, not a professor studying them. I guess it comes down to this: when we're out there I'll follow Kalluk's orders simply because he knows what he's doing—and I don't."

"Yeah. That's the way I see it too. His word and Jessie's are the law for the next couple of weeks or so. Even the brothers agree with that, or they wouldn't be coming along at all." He sighed. "You know . . ." he began and then stopped.

"What?"

"I'm not sure I should tell you this, but I get the feeling Kalluk's pretty interested in you."

"Interested? How?"

R. E. seemed less than comfortable. "It's just that he questions me about you—about your background, how you're taking to Alaska, stuff like that. And what your relationship with me is all about."

"Oh." She sat quietly for a moment. "Well, I don't know that questions like that necessarily mean he's interested in me romantically. After all, I'm going on a field trip with the man."

"I know, I know. It's just that I've heard that the ladies— native women, women at the colleges he visits, women from the small towns—kind of fall all over him." R. E. suddenly

111

seemed not only uncomfortable but embarrassed as well. "I'm . . . look, let's forget it, OK? I don't know what I'm talking about. I'm just rattling on." He stood. "I'd better hit the road. I'd like to get a decent night's sleep tonight, because if I know myself at all, I won't sleep a wink tomorrow night."

"I know what you mean. I probably won't, either. Like my mom used to tell me, 'If patience was a five-dollar bill, you'd be broke.'"

They moved together to the door, R. E. pulling on his heavy coat. They stood in the doorway for a moment, and then Tessa watched from the doorway as R. E. walked to his truck. Fuzz appeared at the corner of the cabin. One moment the wolf-dog wasn't there, the next he was, eyes reflecting R. E.'s headlights just as those of a cat would. Tessa stepped to her kitchen, leaving the door ajar, found half a baloney sandwich in the refrigerator, and returned to the door. She tossed the sandwich out onto the snow. By the time she'd closed the door and walked to the window the treat was gone.

She left the window and collapsed on her couch, suddenly very tired. She sighed, stood again, loaded a pair of good-sized chunks of wood into the woodstove, and returned to the couch. Within a couple of minutes the first wave of new heat washed over her. It felt wonderful.

Tessa's mind replayed parts of the evening. *"I get the feeling Kalluk's pretty interested in you." Nonsense. He seemed more condescending than interested a few hours ago.*

But what about what R. E. said about women falling all over him? Tessa shifted uncomfortably on the couch. Fine. Whatever. But that won't be me.

If that's true, why am I wasting all these thoughts on him?

A bit of trapped moisture in one of the pieces of wood popped, sounding like a loud snap of fingers. Light from the small heat-resistant window of the woodstove flickered for a moment and then settled. The blanket of heat—perhaps a little bit too warm—made Tessa's eyes heavy, and she allowed them to close. The next pop from the fire didn't cause her to stir, nor did the crunch of shifting wood as it burned.

Tessa looked around the small igloo structure, not at all sure when or how they'd built it. The brothers sat on either side of the small entrance/exit, reminding her of the stone lions outside the New York Public Library: solid, unmoving, implacable. Each had a four-inch icicle hanging from the tip of his nose. Their eyes were closed.

Jeopardy! was on the huge wide-screen TV attached to the wall. Alex Trebek was dressed in heavy furs and quite obviously needed a shave; he would have benefited from a shampoo, as well. Puffs of condensation, like the speech balloons in cartoons, floated around him as he said, "The answer is, what anthropologist should have known better than to go on an extended field trip into the wilds with a group of native Alaskans and a storekeeper?"

The camera cut to the contestants: R. E., Kalluk, and Nancy Ehrich, Tessa's graduate assistant from two years ago. Nancy looked stunned. "I'm like . . . ya know?" she babbled.

R. E. buzzed in but said nothing.

Kalluk waved at Alex and said in his Johnny Cash voice, "That's an easy one, Al. That'd be Tessa Rollins, a girl from the lower 48 who . . ."

Tessa sat straight up now and looked around the cabin for the big TV screen and was confused for a moment when she

113

found that it had disappeared. Immediately, her confusion was replaced by almost irrational anger. "The nerve of that guy! Is it my fault I was born in Minnesota? Where does he get off using my name on national TV when he doesn't know a thing about me?"

A soft thud drew her eyes to the window. Fuzz, obviously balanced on his hind legs, was gaping in the window at her, his eyes larger than usual, round with surprise. She met the wolf-dog's eyes with her own, and the contact seemed to last for a long time. Then, Fuzz dropped down and out of sight. Tessa slumped back onto the couch. Her amusement at herself, which began with a chuckle, quickly escalated to full-blown laughter. Fuzz peeked through the window again, eyeing her warily this time, and that made the entire situation even funnier.

***

They met the next day at the mercantile through no particular plan or arrangement. Tessa, Jessie, Albin, Kalluk, and Randall all simply showed up in the early afternoon. The store was quiet. Two Inuit ladies were looking at toaster ovens, and a young girl—the daughter of one of the women—was wistfully eyeing the candy bars in the glass-fronted case near the cash register. R. E. surreptitiously slipped the kid a Baby Ruth and joined the expedition members at the two tables they'd pulled together.

"I see everyone has coffee," he said as he pulled up a chair. "That's strange, because there are no quarters in the self-pay dish."

"The wind probably blew all the change out into the parking lot, where it'll never be found," Jessie suggested.

"That must be it," R. E. agreed. "So, what's up?"

All eyes went to Kalluk. "Everything is as set and ready as it'll ever be," he said. "We'll meet here at about nine so we can start as soon as there's decent light. We'll leave our vehicles out in back by R. E.'s electrical box, where the oil heaters can be plugged in. We load the sleds. Me an' Jessie will do most of that—keeping stuff balanced properly so that it rides OK. Then—we're off."

"I'll carry the battery pack," Jessie said. "We have three good transistor radios for weather reports. We'll divvy those up when we drop the sleds. The med-pack will be in Kalluk's gear, and I'll carry the smaller first-aid kit." She looked around the table. "One thing—I asked Albin and Randall to leave their guns here, told them that I'd bring my 30.06, which would be all we'd need. They said they'd rather leave their boots and go barefoot—or not go at all. So, we'll have a pair of .44 Magnums along with us. Those boys have carried those pistols since they were in moosehide jammies with footies in them. They know what they're doing. I have no problem with it. OK?"

Kalluk grinned. "I think they both still wear those jammies, Jessie."

Jessie ignored him. "Any questions? Concerns? Let's get everything out in the open now, because tomorrow will be too late." She waited for several beats. No one spoke. "Good. We'll have a fine trip. There's one last thing—a tradition. It's how I start all my Alaskan adventures, and something I picked up from my grandparents."

Kalluk's right hand and arm were already extended to the center of the group. Albin and Randall joined him immediately, clutching his hand. Jessie, Tessa, and R. E. followed.

"Good," Jessie said. "We're brothers and sisters in heart, if not in blood. It'll be a good trip."

"I have a tradition too," Tessa said without opening her eyes. "Let's ask the Lord to watch over and protect us, and thank him for the opportunity he's given us to be together and to take this journey."

"Amen," R. E. said.

Tessa was, of course, early, but when she arrived, everyone else was already there behind the mercantile. Jessie and Kalluk had loaded the three small, runnered carriers, and they looked like slightly oversized children's sleds piled—very neatly—with more things than they could logically carry. Albin and Randall stood by drinking coffee from Styrofoam cups, Fuzz standing beside them, as if at attention. R. E. was sliding a carrier to the hitch at the rear of one of the snowmobiles.

Tessa's internal clock was still not completely adjusted to the dusk in the morning season in Alaska. She pulled her Jeep next to R. E.'s truck, facing the block exterior of the back of the mercantile, and clicked off her headlights. She took her crankcase heater from the passenger seat, went to the front of her vehicle, and opened the hood. It was a simple device, the crankcase heater, but an extremely necessary one. It replaced the dipstick that was used for checking the engine oil with a similarly shaped rod that was a basic, low-temp electric heater. Alaskan winter temperatures would turn even the best motor oil to a sludge-like substance with the texture of peanut butter in just a few hours; vehicles parked and not run for a few days wouldn't start. Tessa slammed her hood and uncoiled the electrical wire to the multi-outlet fixture on the wall into which Jessie, Kalluk, and R. E.'s vehicles were already connected.

Tessa hadn't quite known what to expect this morning. Would the group be giddy, their laughter a little loud, as anxious to get going as a bunch of high schoolers leaving on a senior trip? Or would they be subdued, businesslike, already functioning as a team? The actuality, she found, was somewhere in between the extremes. Kalluk and Jessie were highly professional, wasting no motion, performing final checks. Randall, Albin, and Fuzz were as active and helpful as alabaster statues in a frozen garden, and R. E. and Tessa were spending their time getting in the way of or bumping into Kalluk and Jessie.

The morning dusk had given way to a cheerfully blue sky and a generous sun that offered little in the way of warmth but seemed to cleanse the earth and its air of negativity and problems. Kalluk pulled the starter cord on the first snow-mobile, and its engine snarled to life, unmuffled, growling its strength, ready for the adventure. The brothers each drove a heavily packed sled, Kalluk and R. E. rode on another, and Jessie and Tessa on the fourth. Fuzz ranged about the single-file line, loping alongside Kalluk's sled before veering off to explore a scent or a track and then returning to his place next to the snowmobile. The wolf-dog moved with no visible effort, almost gliding over the snow, keeping perfect pace with the lead sled.

Off we go! Tessa thought. *Wait until they hear about this back home—staid, no-nonsense anthro professor Tessa Rollins off on a trek with a pair of handsome guys, two Alaskan natives, a female guide, and a half-wolf.*

The roar of the snowmobile engines became a constant drone in Tessa's world—and then it receded so that she was no more conscious of it than a long-time dweller on a lake is aware of the sound of waves sloughing against the beach. Jessie controlled the snowmobile expertly, holding a position about twenty-five feet behind Kalluk and R. E. The air was crisp, crystalline, without wind or even a breeze. When Kalluk's sled powered through a drift, the snow seemed to hang in the air, glittering like tiny gems in the bright sunlight, as if it were in no hurry to return to the ground.

Tessa, after a few miles, relaxed a bit, loosening the death grip she'd used to clutch the sides of Jessie's coat, leaning back slightly to ease her back, riding with the motion of the sled, as a good rider does on her mount. The seat itself was lightly padded and was more comfortable than a hewn beam but less comfortable than an office chair. The saving grace was that Jessie had placed waterproof heating wires through the padding, and although not a great deal of warmth was provided, the difference was quite noticeable—and appreciated.

By the time they'd traveled an hour and a half, all signs of Fairview and civilization were gone; the tundra, the lines of snow-laden trees, and the smooth grace of wind-created snow sculpture extended to forever around them.

Jessie reached back and handed Tessa a Hershey bar—the large size, with almonds. Tess tugged her mittens off with her teeth, unwrapped the candy bar, stuffed the paper and aluminum foil into her pocket, and held the bar between her teeth as she put her mittens back on. She hadn't realized that she was so hungry, but the first sweet taste of the chocolate melting in her mouth was a catalyst that started her stomach rumbling. *Chocolate and caffeine—what could possibly be better? But why am I so hungry? All I've been doing is sitting here looking at the scenery and the back of Jessie's head. Maybe it's the cold working. Just carrying on normal metabolic stuff in intense cold burns a ton of calories, doesn't it?* She grinned. *Instant diet! What a great way to advertise my course at the university: be an anthropologist! Get rid of flabby thighs! No more buffalo butt! No exercise, no special meals, and no calorie counting. Anthropology—the major of the svelte and sexy.*

She pushed the balance of the chocolate bar into her mouth and rubbed her itching nose vigorously with the back of her mitten. She glanced at the back of her left wrist—which was covered by the sleeve of her insulated long underwear shirt, her sweater, and the last couple of inches of the sleeve of her coat—from habit. Tessa's watch, a Geneva her folks gave to her on her graduation from high school, was in a drawer back in her cabin. Kalluk had suggested that she leave it behind because it could be damaged and because standard time would have little or no meaning to the group. Tess noticed that Jessie didn't wear a watch. She'd never seen the wrists of Albin and Randall, but she suspected that watches would be as likely a part of their daily wear as Mickey Mouse ears. R. E. had left his trusty Timex at home. She'd often wondered why he bothered with it at all. He opened and closed the mercantile pretty much when he cared to, and gauged commitments by "this afternoon" or "tomorrow morning."

The motion of Kalluk's arm rising brought Tessa back to the trip from wherever it was that her mind had taken her. The droning of the engines and the sweep of what appeared to be an unchanging panorama of snow around them had a hypnotic effect, a sort of monotony that made mind-drifting almost impossible to avoid.

Kalluk slowed to a stop, followed by the other sleds. Jessie pushed herself to her feet and thudded her boots against the snow-covered ground. Tessa swung a leg over the sled and was surprised to find herself sitting ungracefully in the snow. She attempted to right herself and found that her legs weren't cooperating. Albin, who'd come up behind her, extended an arm. Tess grabbed it and pulled herself to her feet. Her legs tingled their entire length. Albin leaned close to her—exactly as if he were about to kiss her—and eyed her face closely.

"Nose," he said.

"Nose?"

Tessa touched her nose with her mitten and found that there was very little sensation in it. She began to scratch it on the back of her mitten. Albin grunted and grabbed her forearm. Jessie leaned in next to Albin. "Cover your face below your eyes with a scarf when we set out again, Tess," she said. "You've got some frostbite started. It'll be OK, but whatever you do, don't rub or scratch at it." Albin let go of her arm and walked over to where Kalluk, R. E., and Randall were crouched. Fuzz was next to them, his tail moving back and forth slowly, his eyes riveted to the small butcher-paper package his master was unwrapping. Kalluk tossed a bloody chunk of meat about the size of a plucked chicken into the air; Fuzz snatched it and hustled off a few yards to gnaw on his treat.

"It's an elk heart," Kalluk said to Tessa as she walked toward him, her legs still shaky. "Lots of protein. He loves them—good for him too. I had this one kind of hanging around in R. E.'s freezer, so I figured I might as well bring it along for ol' Fuzz."

Tessa did her best to control her disgust, to not let it show on her face. Kalluk noticed her unsteady shuffle. "You've got to move your legs and feet or they'll set up on you when you're riding for a long time," he said. He turned back to the shoe-box-sized propane stove he was adjusting, sparked a throw-away lighter, and smiled as the circular burner caught. "Coffee in a few minutes—food a few minutes later," he said.

R. E. touched Tessa lightly on the arm. "Let's walk a little—get the blood flowing to your legs. Mine set up a bit too. C'mon."

"Good idea." Tess smiled. "But I'm not moving a step until I have a cup of very hot coffee in my hand." A battered old percolator pot began to gurgle over the propane flames, and, simultaneous with the sounds, the earthy, delightful aroma of fresh-brewed coffee suffused the air around the group. Even the brothers moved closer to Kalluk's stove, savoring the scent. Jessie handed out army-style tin cups. "Everybody gets one of these, and only one. Lose it, crush it, whatever, and you'll drink coffee and soup from a tin can." She looked around at the others. "Understood?" Albin and Randall nodded. Tessa, Kalluk, and R. E. murmured affirmatively.

That makes sense, Tessa thought. *Jessie's done this sort of thing many times, and she knows how a field trip has to run. Experience is the best teacher.* R. E. caught her eye for a moment and nodded, and she saw his thoughts were much the same.

They walked together, sipping their coffee, cradling the cups two-handed to draw the heat into their fingers and palms. "Legs feeling better?" R. E. asked.

"Much. We've barely started, and I've learned something: move my legs as much as possible while a passenger on a snowmobile."

"Me too. I wonder how far we've come? It seems like we've been riding forever."

Tessa looked around. "I don't know how to estimate distance when everything looks pretty much the same. Even time out here seems different, like it moves slower, somehow. It's as if . . . hey! What's that?"

Fifty yards ahead of them, on a slight rise near a stand of pines, the snow exploded from the ground. There was a sharp, almost feminine-sounding scream, and then silence. The snow settled on Fuzz's back as he stood, head down, with blotches of crimson around his mouth.

"Fuzz got a rabbit," R. E. said. "You wouldn't think he'd be hungry after that huge heart he ate."

Tessa shuddered, and the cold wasn't the cause. "That horrible scream—that was a rabbit? I didn't know . . ."

"Yeah. Awful sound, isn't it? I wonder what Fuzz is doing out here, though. He usually sticks pretty close to Kalluk."

"I need to stop thinking of Fuzz as I think of dogs back home," Tessa admitted. "He's not like them at all."

R. E. stopped and looked back toward the sleds, which were now hidden from view behind a gentle rise. "Maybe he'll grow on you, Tess." He grinned at her. "We should probably get back. Those MREs don't take long to heat, and I'm starved."

"Me too," Tessa agreed. "And it might be a good idea for us to keep the others in sight when we're out walking, you know? Like I said, everything looks the same. If we wandered too far we'd be in trouble."

R. E. nodded. "Good point. Let's do that from now on." He touched Tessa's shoulder, and she stopped and turned to him. "This is great, isn't it? Being out here, in the real Alaska."

Tess smiled up at him. "It *is* great, R. E. I'm glad we're here." She looked beyond R. E. Fuzz was watching them from his place on the little hill, the partially devoured carcass of the rabbit hanging from his mouth. There was some distance between so Tessa wasn't quite sure—but it looked like the wolf-dog's tail was waving gently as he looked at her. She held the eye contact for a moment longer. *I guess I've found a half-wild friend,* she thought. For whatever reason, the thought pleased her. "We'd better get back," she said. "No sense in being late for our first meal on the tundra."

The MREs weren't half bad—not culinary art, but hot, filling, and semi-tasty. Tessa finished her beef ravioli, scooping it directly from the heating pouch with a tablespoon she'd carried in her backpack, just as Jessie had instructed her to do. Kalluk poured an inch or so of the remaining coffee into each of their cups, used handfuls of snow to clean the pot, shut down the propane stove, and repacked everything. He stepped to the front of his sled and pulled the starter cord. The engine snarled to life immediately.

"Ready?" he asked.

Within a few minutes the sleds were once again in the positions they'd occupied since the trip began, Fuzz loping along effortlessly slightly behind Kalluk.

Tessa, her thick woolen scarf wrapped securely around her face and her hat pulled down over her eyebrows, watched the passing terrain from the one-inch slot between the scarf and her hat. The temperature, she noticed, was dropping, just as the quality of the light was decreasing. The short Alaska winter day was beginning to end. Shadows grew longer and deeper, and a new wind toyed with the snow, frisking it into the air randomly, leaving some patches untouched, creating white whirlwinds of others. In the group of five other people and amid the blare of the sled engines, Tessa was alone with her thoughts.

There was something different about R. E. a while ago, when we walked before our meal. When Fuzz killed that rabbit there was sympathy in his eyes for the bunny, but there was something else there too—something different, or maybe something I never really saw before. Have I been a bit quick in thinking of him as simply a buddy?

Kalluk waved his arm to get the other drivers' attention and pulled in a long, gentle arc to what appeared to be the edge of a forest. He stopped until the other snowmobiles caught up to him, turned on his headlamp, and entered the woods at walking speed, snow squealing under the treads louder than the grumble of his engine. Jessie and the brothers flicked on their lights and followed Kalluk.

Kalluk stopped near a pair of fallen trees and snugged his snowmobile close to them. He and R. E. stood while the other sleds shut down. "There's enough light left to find firewood," Kalluk said. "Let's get to it."

"Wait," Jessie said. "How about Albin, Randall, and R. E. go for firewood and the three of us set up the tents? The light's fading fast."

It was clear from Kalluk's quick change in posture—from casual to a military tightness—that he didn't like having his order countermanded. Nevertheless, after a tense moment, he said, "Yeah. Good point."

Tessa had seen the MontBell tents before, of course, and she'd even practiced setting one up. Still, the size and lightness of the two-person tents that would be the group's sole protection against the power of an arctic winter, amazed her. The Osprey mountaineering backpacks that R. E. had gotten using his dealer discount were much the same: they weighed slightly over two pounds and were very comfortable to wear, yet could carry a truly amazing amount of trekking necessities.

Kalluk started the fire from bits of kindling and quickly added brush to it as the others hauled wood to the camp. Soon it was bonfire size, crackling cheerfully, orange-red flames leaping into the night, waves of heat rolling outward, shimmering in the frigid air. Kalluk helped Tessa position the tents in an arc with the zippered openings facing the fire. They worked efficiently together, almost wordlessly. There were plenty of rocks about, and it didn't take long to secure the bases of the tents against the wind with them.

Randall, carrying a log that probably weighed two hundred pounds, stopped in front of Kalluk and said something Tessa couldn't hear. "Nah," Kalluk answered. "MREs tonight—the more of them we eat the fewer we have to carry. There'll always be game around."

Randall nodded, dropped his log next to the fire, and went back out into the rapidly deepening night.

Tessa looked questioningly at Kalluk.

"The brothers don't much care for prepared food," Kalluk explained. "A couple of five- or six-pound rabbits make a great meal. There's no need for hunting quite yet, though." He pulled the log Randall had just left closer to the fire, to serve as a sort of bench. "Let's get the coffee on," he said.

"The guys hauling wood will have our heads if the brew isn't ready when they're done."

Jessie was using a small Maglite to check the fuel gauges of the four snowmobiles. She pulled the oil dipstick on each as well and carefully inspected the level. "We're in good shape on fuel," she called to Kalluk. "Plenty of miles left before we have to leave the sleds. Oil's good too."

Tessa watched the coffeepot as if it were going to run away; she clutched her cup in her mittened hands. Kalluk eased down on the log next to her and nudged a piece of wood that hadn't yet caught closer to the flames with his boot. "How's your nose feel?" he asked.

If it'd felt like a tiger was chewing on it, Tessa wouldn't have said so. "Not bad at all," she said, taking off her scarf. "Jessie said I caught it in time. Itches a bit," she added.

"Good. That's good." For moments the only sounds were the beginning gasps of the coffeepot, the crunching of snow and cracking of branches from the wood-gathering detail, and Jessie sorting MREs and humming quietly to herself. "What do you think so far, Tessa?" Kalluk asked.

Tessa considered. "Well, I haven't yet spent a night in the wilds, but I've enjoyed every minute since we left Fairview. I know that you and Jessie and the brothers have done this a gazillion times, but to me and R. E. it's an adventure of a lifetime."

"It's always an adventure," Kalluk said seriously. "No two trips are ever the same. And this one is especially important to me."

"Because of the meeting with the People?"

"Yeah—at least partially. And it's nice to have another woman along, someone who cares about the same things I do." Kalluk spoke normally, without nervousness, as if he'd just commented on how comfortable his wool socks were. Nevertheless, the compliment flustered Tessa.

"That's kind of you to say, Kalluk," she said.

"Maybe. But it's true too."

R. E. trudged up to the camp and dumped an armload of branches and larger pieces onto the firewood pile. "Yo! Is the coffee ready yet?" he called out. "Getting cold out there—I don't know if I want to drink the coffee or soak my feet in it!"

Kalluk stood, apparently finished with his conversation with Tessa. "I'd be careful about the feet thing, R. E.—this java is strong enough to melt a horseshoe. You might pull out a couple of stumps."

The brothers drifted into the camp, dropped off their firewood, and tugged a hefty log to the fire, a few feet from where Tessa sat. Jessie and R. E. sat with Tessa; Kalluk poured coffee into the waiting cups. That done, he began arranging MRE plates on the periphery of the fire. Finally, he hunkered down between the two seating logs, in a seemingly uncomfortable bent-knee position Tessa had seen Inuits employ before. She made a mental note: *Perhaps something to look into as a cultural attribute?*

"Seems somebody here has a thing for Tessa," Kalluk said, laughter in his voice. Eyes swung to him and then to and beyond Tess, where Kalluk was pointing. Fuzz sat a yard behind Tessa, staring at the back of her head, as still and unmoving as an ice sculpture, the pale green of his eyes luminous in the light of the fire. Tessa turned to look, and her hand rose reflexively, protectively, to her throat. "What does he want?" she asked.

127

"Not a thing," Kalluk assured her. "These guys will do that sometimes, pick out a friend for their own reasons. It's strange—the friend is often someone who either is afraid of them or just plain doesn't like them."

"Like cats always choosing to jump into the lap of someone who's either allergic to them or dislikes them," R. E. said.

Tessa looked away from the wolf-dog. His eyes hadn't moved, and she could sense his focus on her as she turned. "I don't dislike Fuzz," she said. "And I'm not afraid of him, either—not really. I'm just not used to wolf-dogs. It's not like there were packs of them back in Minnesota, you know."

"Actually," Kalluk said, "I've heard about timber wolves in Minnesota. There are—"

"There are *canis lupus*, and they're a good deal smaller than Fuzz. Once in a while they'll take a lamb or a calf, but they pretty much exist on rodents and snakes and roadkill," Jessie said.

All eyes turned to her.

She sipped her coffee. "I read *National Geographic*," she said. "There was an article a couple of months ago on Minnesota."

"I can see that this trip is going to be an educational experience we'll never forget," R. E. said, forced awe apparent in his voice. "Wow! *Canis lupus*!"

"Knucklehead," Jessie said.

—◦•⊱⊰•◦—

The fire cast its orangeish yellow glow for a good distance around itself, suffusing the snow with soft light, washing the sharp edges from shadows nearby. The air was completely still; smoke from the fire rose ruler-straight into the night sky. Albin and Randall sat motionless, Indian style, at the very edge of the glow. If they spoke, their voices were so quiet that no one else could hear them. Tessa decided that they weren't speaking; they were simply being together, just as they had been for all their lives. Other than Albin's cautioning her about her nose, Tessa hadn't seen the brothers exchange a word between themselves or with anyone else all day. A quirky thought struck her: *How much of what passes for conversation—chitchat—in the lower 48 is really worth breaking silence for? How many of us can sit with someone who's important to us, someone we love, without feeling the need to clutter up the time with inconsequential words?*

Tessa and R. E. walked slowly together, well within the firelight. Kalluk was sitting outside a tent, sharpening a sheath knife with a rectangle of stone, working the blade lightly against it, the slight scritch-scritch sound rhythmic and clear in the quiet. Jessie peered into the embers at the edge of the fire, motionless, looking to be a thousand miles away.

"Your legs still a little stiff?" R. E. asked Tessa.

"A little. Walking eases them up."

Fuzz glided by a few yards to their side, moving in the smooth, flowing motion that seemed to be part of his nature.

"I guess we're going to have lots of time to think on this trip, Tess. Even on this first day, I've been rolling things around in my mind."

"I know what you mean. And that'll probably be even more true once we leave the snowmobiles and start hiking. There'll be no noise and no fast motion—just the sound of scrunching snow." She had the feeling that R. E. had more to say, that his earlier comments weren't without some meaning to them. "What've you been rolling around in your head?" she asked.

They took a couple of steps before R. E. answered. "I guess nothing specific. A kind of analysis of stuff."

"Stuff?"

"Yeah. How much I'm enjoying all this, what'll happen after we get back and the trip is all finished, things like that." They took another step. "What'll you do then, Tess?"

The question perplexed her for a moment. "Hmmm. I'll finish up my writing, I suppose. Visit the elders with Meeloa a few more times. Then, head on back to Minnesota and the university with some very fond memories."

"And lots of photographs too."

"Sure. Lots of pictures of all of us from the trip and the People and the store and my cabin . . . and everything."

"That'll be good," R. E. said quietly. He stopped, and Tessa stopped next to him. R. E. tilted his head upward. "Look," he said, raising his arm. A shooting star flashed across the sky, its tail bright and wide and distinct, even among the pure light of billions of other stars. Tessa followed it with her eyes.

Then, R. E. was in front of her—and then he was kissing her, his lips warm against hers.

8

The first night in a tent and a sleeping bag in the Alaskan wilds was more comfortable than Tessa had expected it to be. She'd tried the sleeping bag on the floor of her cabin and found it amazingly warm, although it didn't do much to soften the hardness of the floor. Now, the bottom of the sleeping bag was on the tent's space-age floor sheet, and under that was snow that conformed, at least slightly, to her body. Sleeping in such close proximity to another person was a new experience; every time Jessie moved, Tessa jolted awake. That, she assured herself, would soon end.

Tessa heard motion outside the tent a few inches from her face. Then, the fabric of the tent bulged inward at the ground level. She put out a tentative hand—and felt the shoulder muscle of Fuzz, or at least she hoped it was Fuzz. The satisfied grunt of the wolf-dog as she touched him through the fabric told Tessa it was her new friend. She pulled her arm back into the cocoon of the sleeping bag and tucked the inner cover over most of her head. She was deliciously warm and safe and very tired, but her mind didn't seem to want to slow down enough to allow her to drift back to sleep.

The walk and conversation with R. E.—and the sudden, unanticipated kiss—played in a loop in her mind, and each time around, her emotions ranged from mild astonishment to a strange and a quite new interest in this man. *Have I been misreading R. E.? He's not the type of guy to grab a quick kiss for the fun of it. I know him enough to understand that—but how well do I really know him? He's a storekeeper with a strange name who loves Alaska—but what else? Is it possible that he cares for me and I've been too absorbed in everything else in my life to be aware of his feelings? And—what are my feelings? One tiny kiss doesn't change anything. Does it?*

The lump that was Fuzz's side shifted and then was gone. For a moment Tessa heard his pads squeaking on the snow, and then the silence of the night returned.

Tessa recalled one of her conversations with Meeloa about Alaskan men and lower 48 expatriates who'd become Alaskan men. *"Some of these guys, Tess—they're kind of like the men in the American West in the 1880s—the ones hack writers tell about in Western action novels. They're haunted in a sense, not by ghost-type nonsense, but by the fact that everything around them is changing too fast. Look how some Inuit men and some new Alaskans live. They spend most of their time in the wilds, hunting, fishing, all that—because they're trying to hold on to something that's creeping away. Or, find something here that's already gone from where they came from."* She'd hesitated for a bit before going on. *"R. E.'s like that, I think. In a sense, he's not a store clerk. He's a seeker, and he's found pretty much what he was looking for."*

When Tessa awoke, the light had that gray, grainy texture that told her it was what passed for morning during the winter season. What had drawn her from sleep was the scent of brewing coffee and the murmur of voices outside her tent. Jessie, she saw, was already up and out; she hadn't heard a sound from her tent mate, even as Jessie rolled up her sleeping bag and pulled on her boots and coat. Tessa moved the cover away from her face and took a deep breath. The air was sharply cold, and her sleeping bag offered her a wondrously secure way to beat the frigidity. All she needed to do was stay inside it forever.

She reached an arm out of the warmth, tugged down the zipper, and sat up, pushing her hair back off her forehead and face. She pulled on her boots, which were as warm and welcoming as a pair of blocks of ice, and wrestled her long coat over the jeans and shirt and two layers of thermal underwear she'd slept in. She pushed open the entrance to the tent, stooped a bit, and stepped through.

The first thing she saw in the murky light was Kalluk and Randall, each holding a cup of coffee and gazing down at the snow in front of her tent. Her eyes followed theirs, and she yelped as if she'd stepped on something sharp that pierced her boot and cut into her foot. She stood in place, still slightly crouched, and stared at the dead, torn-open rabbit that rested in a patch of darkness on the snow that she knew was the creature's blood.

"I've never seen anything like this," Kalluk was saying, something bordering on awe in his voice.

"Me neither," Randall said. "Not for nobody but owner."

Tessa forced herself to look down at the rabbit again. "Fuzz?" she asked.

133

Kalluk nodded. "Yeah. A little gift for you."

Randall grinned broadly. "He don't eat good parts, either. Leave you heart, liver."

"Swell," Tessa mumbled as she stepped away toward the fire that was already blazing. "Can you guys please get rid of that poor thing?"

Randall grunted, "I take," before Kalluk could speak.

Kalluk moved to Tessa's side at the fire. "At least the meat won't be wasted," he said. "It's really strange, though. I've never seen a wolf-dog offer food to anyone other than his owner. They're one-man creatures. It just doesn't happen."

"I wonder why he chose me?" Tessa asked. "I haven't made overtures to him. All I did was give him some scraps the night he stayed outside my cabin."

"I dunno. Maybe it's your charm that got him."

"Must be," Tessa said. She pulled her army cup from her coat pocket, and Kalluk took it gently from her hand. He crouched, filled the cup with steaming coffee, stood, and handed it to Tessa.

"You'll get used to stuff like that," he said, nodding toward the bloody rabbit. "Or, if not used to it, at least inured. And, I think it's a good thing Fuzz is watching out for you. Out here, you couldn't have a better friend."

Tessa sipped her coffee. It was still too hot to drink, but it tasted wonderful. "Where is he now? Is he around?"

"He's always around. You want me to whistle him up?"

"Yeah. Please."

Kalluk put his thumb and forefinger together and brought his hand to his mouth. He didn't appear to blow particularly hard, but the whistle he produced was high-pitched and loud enough to make Tessa want to press her mittens against her ears. For a long moment, nothing happened. Then, Fuzz loped his way through an opening in the trees, gliding without effort, his pads barely disturbing the snow. He slowed to a trot fifteen feet away from Kalluk and walked the last short distance. He sat with his eyes fixed on his owner.

Tessa stepped closer to Kalluk. "Fuzz," she said.

The wolf-dog didn't turn his head toward her until Kalluk made a small motion with the fingers of his right hand. Then, Fuzz turned to Tessa, his tail beginning to sweep back and forth a few inches. She stopped in front of him and extended her hand. She touched Fuzz very lightly between the ears, her eyes riveted to his. Other than the increasing sweep of his tail, the animal was motionless. There were some crystals of ice on his muzzle, she saw, and the texture of the fur on his head was softer than she expected, and thick. She crouched slightly and let her hand trail down his neck to his shoulder. Fuzz's muscles were firm under his luxurious coat, but not actually hard—pliable, and powerful, like the leg muscles of a marathon runner.

"Ummm . . . nice boy," Tessa said, feeling foolish the moment she heard her own words. Kalluk's quiet laugh increased her embarrassment. Jessie, walking over from where she'd been packing her snowmobile, stopped and watched for a moment.

"Well," she said, "it's about time. I knew that handsome ol' critter'd win you over, Tessa." When Tessa looked at the older woman she saw a broad smile.

Kalluk made another tiny hand motion. Fuzz rose, backed up a step with his eyes still fixed on Tessa, turned, and eased off toward the thicker woods. The brothers, who'd been setting MREs on the edges of the fire to heat, both nodded to Tessa.

The log that had served as a bench the evening before had been pushed into the fire a bit at a time by the men through the night, and less than a foot of it remained unburned. The group stood about, forking their food from the pans, gazing into the sputtering remains of the fire, and enjoying the final heat it provided.

"Kalluk says we'll drop the sleds in a few hours," R. E. said as he walked over to Tessa. "The GPS will pinpoint where we stash them, and it'll be no sweat picking them up on the way back." He laughed. "Funny—before this, I didn't even know that global positioning systems worked anywhere but on roads with distinct reference points."

"I never gave it much thought," Tessa admitted. "But Jessie swears by them, and that's good enough for me."

"Me too. Well, I gotta start the sleds, let the engines idle. See you a little later, OK? Lunchtime?"

"You bet." Tessa watched R. E.'s back as he strode toward the snowmobiles. *He seemed a little nervous, but we're back to normal—whatever normal is.*

Kalluk, in his usual way of suddenly and silently appearing when he wasn't expected, stood to Tessa's side. "Gathering wool?" he asked.

"I guess so. Lost in thought for a minute."

Kalluk stood comfortably near her, not infringing on her personal space but yet close enough for quiet conversation. "I'm really glad you're along," he said.

She smiled. "You mentioned that before. But thanks, so am I."

"I guess I did say that yesterday, didn't I? It's still true, though." There was no embarrassment in his face. "You kind of make me think of what I may have become if I didn't go the way I did. A teacher, and academic, I mean. I'd reach a whole lot more people."

"Maybe a higher number of people. But never assume that all students are in the classrooms to learn what the professors teach. Some are filling requirements, some are looking for an easy grade, some are there because they had an opening in their schedule and needed the credit hours."

"I'm sure that's true. But I get to talk to the people who come to see me for an hour or so and then answer some questions. You get to stand there class after class, semester after semester. You said some students don't really care what you're teaching, but a good number of them must care, right?"

"Sure. Lots of them do, and it's fulfilling to work with them."

"So you get your message out."

Tessa considered that for a moment. "Yeah, I do. Tell me, Kalluk, what's your message? Why do you do what you do? What got you started as an advocate?"

Kalluk had turned his head slightly at a sound from the woods, but his eyes found Tessa's quickly once again. "I was raised by my grandparents. My mother died giving birth to me. She was very young—and unmarried. They were all native Inuits. So, her folks took me in. My great-grandfather lived in the traditional way and stopped at my grandparents' home a couple times a year. I loved that man, loved the life he was living. If he'd have asked, I'd have gone with him without a thought."

"He told you about the traditional ways, then."

137

"Oh yeah," Kalluk said. "He sure did. He was a storyteller, Tessa. And the more stories he told me, the more I loved him and his life. He spoke of my heritage, but I didn't really understand what he meant until I was twelve or thirteen. That was the year of his last trip—the last time I saw him. He told me that because of my love for what he'd told me all my life, it was my duty to the People to, well . . . spread to others, particularly native people . . . the ways of the elders, so that they'd never be forgotten."

The intensity of Kalluk's eyes, the depths of the brown-black pupils, the powerful directness of his gaze, actually made Tessa slightly dizzy. "I see," she said. "And that's why—"

The clattering roar of a snowmobile engine broke into Tessa's thoughts. Within a few moments, another sled started, and then another. Tessa leaned closer to Kalluk, speaking directly into his ear. "I'd like to hear more," she said.

"And you will. You can count on that."

❖❖❖

They rode for four hours or so, Kalluk and R. E. in the lead, Jessie and Tessa next, and Albin and Randall in their individual sleds hanging last. Fuzz ran next to the lead snow-mobile most of the time, breaking off to explore an interesting track or scent every so often. When Kalluk gestured for a stop, the party was ready for coffee and food.

Tessa unwrapped her scarf from her face and bent at the waist, easing tense muscles, and then kneaded her lower back with her hands. She'd shifted the position of her legs frequently on this ride; she walked easily and comfortably alongside Jessie toward where Kalluk was setting up the propane stove.

"It seems colder than yesterday," Tessa observed.

"It is," Jessie said. "Spit."

"What?"

"Go ahead—spit."

Tessa turned her back self-consciously, gathered some saliva in her mouth, and spit. There was a tiny sound, like that of a small twig snapping. Tessa's spittle froze in midair, well before it struck the ground. "Wow," Tessa breathed.

Kalluk set the coffeepot on the little stove and stood. "Listen up, Tess and R. E.," he said. "We're getting into some really cold temperatures. You probably know this already, but I'm going to tell it to you again: don't exert yourself for any reason, and breathe in only through your nose. If you start gulping this air—from running or whatever—it'll damage your lungs as badly as inhaling flames would." He looked at R. E. and then at Tessa. "Understood?"

"Sure," R. E. said.

"Good." Kalluk addressed the entire group now. "We're doing OK on gas," he said. "I suggest we heat some soup here and go on until we have to stop to secure the sleds. We can make a fire there and eat before we set off on foot."

Jessie checked the sky before answering. "Maybe we should make camp where we leave the snowmobiles," she said. "We've made good time so far, and a couple hours won't make any difference. After all, this isn't a race."

Kalluk didn't seem to like the plan, but he had to admit that it made sense. "How about this, then—we skip the soup for now and keep on hauling and then make a night camp later, like you said."

Tessa grimaced inwardly but let nothing show on her face. The idea of hot soup—even from a powder mix—had

139

sounded heavenly to her. Kalluk took the silence of the others as acceptance and leaned down to shut off the propane stove. "Let's get moving, then," he said.

The snowmobiles droned onward. The terrain was a vast whiteness broken only by the occasional stand of pines, jutting boulders, and slopes and valleys that seemed invisible to Tessa when they were in the distance, noticeable only as the sleds passed over them. They skirted a forest that seemed to go on forever, unchanging, the snow-shrouded trees no different from one another than grains of sand on a beach. Once, Tessa saw a dozen or so elk in the distance, and the beauty of the creatures took her breath away. Closer game, she realized, had run from the racket of the engines.

Tessa's mind entered into a state of almost thoughtless lethargy. It was a non-time, like what Tessa imagined it'd be like to be hypnotized. It was an uncomplicated and quite tranquil sensation.

Everything changed in less than an instant.

Jessie swerved the snowmobile violently to her left and at the same time cranked the throttle wide open. The engine howled, and the right side of the sled rose a foot off the snow as the machine blasted under full power into the too-abrupt turn. Over the scream of the engine Tessa heard Jessie's yell: "Kalluk, ice!" The sled under Tessa slammed down on its treads and ground to a halt, a rooster-tail of snow behind it. Before forward motion halted, Jessie was off the snowmobile and running toward the rear of Kalluk and R. E.'s machine.

Tessa stood gaping at the scrambling Jessie and then at the other sled, which was still moving forward, its speed and direction unchanged. Then, the snowmobile disappeared. In its place was a jagged ten-foot oval of dark, churning water littered with chunks of ice.

Albin and Randall rocketed past Tessa and slowed to a stop where Jessie stood. Both men were off the snowmobile before the engine died. Albin took slow, measured, extremely careful steps toward the gaping hole in the ice. Randall grabbed a coil of rope from the trailer their sled towed, took a wrap around the front of the sled, and hurled the rest of the rope to his brother. His throw was perfect. Albin gathered the slack from the rope, formed a quick loop, and took another step. The silence—the abrupt transition from the bellow of four powerful engines to the profound quiet of the wilds—was almost overwhelming. It was as if Kalluk and R. E.'s snowmobile had sucked all the sound in the world with it when it plunged into the frigid water.

Tessa gawked woodenly at Jessie and Randall, her mind refusing to accept what she'd just witnessed. Jessie's shouted, "Tessa—get a tent up! Move!" jolted her into motion. She rushed back to the sled and pawed through the trailer, tossing MREs and bits of clothing aside as she freed a tent and began to erect it. Her hands trembled and fumbled with the fabric and the metal rods. "Easy, Tess," Jessie called. "Slow down. Don't panic. We'll get them out. Bring the tent over here. When it's up, get together all the clothing you can and put it inside."

Albin began another shuffling step and then stopped in midmotion. What halted him began as a cracking/popping rumble that quickly escalated to the sound of metal being torn apart by some gigantic power. A lightning-like rip appeared in the snow and ice, beginning at the point where Kalluk's sled had gone down, slashing its way past

Albin, and opening a channel of a few inches in width. Albin eased back.

At that moment, Kalluk's head popped to the surface of the water. His face was a chalky white and his lips a dull blue against the pallor. His hat was gone, and his hair looked like it was frozen to his head. He opened his mouth, but no sound came forth. An instant later R. E.'s head appeared an arm's length from Kalluk. Fuzz came to the surface last, his paws flailing at the water.

Albin, his movements calm and controlled, whirled the loop over his head once and flung it the twenty or so feet to the floundering men. Kalluk snatched at the rope with clumsy hands and began to put it over R. E.'s shoulders.

"No!" Albin shouted. Kalluk looked at him, trying to form words through his now violently chattering teeth. "No!" Albin yelled again and held up two fingers. Kalluk managed a nod and widened the loop, so that it went under R. E.'s arms. Then Kalluk fit it over himself in the same way.

Randall and Jessie were already running when the rope settled near Kalluk. Jessie piled into the driver's position of the sled the rope was attached to, and Randall yanked the starter cord. The engine fired, and Jessie eased the snowmobile forward toward Randall, who was walking backward now, a few feet from the sled, motioning Jessie onward. The rope tightened, and the sled hesitated against the load, its tread churning snow as oily exhaust tainted the still air.

Bits and shards of ice popped off the rope as it became taut. Jessie feathered the throttle and watched Randall's hand for instructions. Kalluk and R. E. moved ponderously through the chunks of ice like an awkward ship pushing its way through floes to a safe port.

Tessa ducked back into the tent she'd erected and began to sort the armfuls of clothing she'd tossed inside. "Make it easy for them," she mumbled to herself. She separated jeans, shirts, sweaters, long underwear, and socks into piles, regardless of size or ownership. She realized it was essential—literally a matter of life or death—that the men get out of their soaked and frozen clothes as quickly as possible and into dry garments.

Tessa stepped out of the tent and focused on the rescue. Fuzz had scrambled out of the water and onto the precarious surface of the ice, but rather than dashing to safety he slipped and skidded about the edges of the fissure. He barked in his strange wolf-dog voice, frantic as Kalluk was drawn toward him.

The snowmobile bogged down for a moment as the two men were pulled to the edge of the ice. Jessie hit the throttle, and the sled sprang forward. Kalluk and R. E. seemed to erupt from the water and were airborne for a half-heartbeat before they slammed to the frozen surface. Jessie opened the throttle wide, and the two men bounded and banged their way over the snow to solid land.

The moment the men were on safe ground Jessie jammed the shift lever into neutral and ran to Kalluk and R. E. Randall freed the rope from the front of the sled, piled into the driver's position, and raced toward the distant tree line. Albin, again placing his feet and his weight cautiously, made his way to shore and freed the now stiff and frozen rope from his friends. Then he and Jessie began dragging the two to the tent. Tessa ran to help, and they muscled and skidded R. E. and Kalluk into the tent. Wordlessly, Albin joined them inside and tugged the flap closed behind him.

Fuzz's canine—or lupine—instincts told him to roll in the snow to break away the cocoon of ice that held him prisoner. He dug his shoulders deep as the rest of his body writhed and twisted, and the snapping of ice from his coat made popcorn-like sounds. When he got to his feet and shook his body, much like a retriever coming out of water, crystalline snippets flew from his coat. He appeared none the worse for the dousing.

"Use my propane stove to melt some snow, Tessa," Jessie instructed. "There's a pound of sugar at the bottom of our trailer. When the water's hot, mix sugar—a lot of it—into the water. These guys need the body heat the sugar will generate. Randall will be back with—"

The blare of a snowmobile engine under full power cut into Jessie's words. "Here he comes with wood. We'll get a fire going. You take care of that sugar water."

Tessa dug through the trailer, grabbed Jessie's stove—the same kind Kalluk had—and then found the sugar in a brown paper bag enclosed in a baggie. In moments she had the stove burning and had crammed a small pot full of snow. She continued adding handfuls of snow as the original mass melted; the stuttering of the stove and the quiet hiss of the heating water were the most important things in her universe just now.

Randall roared up to the tent, his sled piled with a precarious mound of firewood. He and Jessie built a rough pyramid, and Jessie crouched with kindling at its base. The minuscule lick of fire Jessie touched to it grew quickly into hungry flames leaping at the sky.

The scene of Kalluk, R. E., Fuzz, and the snowmobile disappearing so suddenly into the dark pit of frigid water repeated in Tessa's mind until she chased it away with a prayer. *Please, Lord—these are good men. You've let them be taken from the water, and I beg you now to warm their bodies.* She adjusted the flame on the stove and added more snow. The frightening tableau returned to her mind.

Suppose Albin didn't know what to do, hadn't gotten out there with the rope? How long could they have lasted in that water? How long can a human body survive anything that cold? What if they couldn't find the hole in the ice after they went down? Can we get a plane or a helicopter in here to take them to a hospital? Suppose . . . suppose . . .

Lord, it's in your hands now, just as everything earthly is and always has been. Please, Lord, let R. E. and Kalluk feel the warmth of your hand on them.

Albin had pitched Kalluk and R. E.'s clothing outside the tent, where it now rested in a gray, frozen heap. Tessa hustled to the tent, freed their outer coats from the pile with a sound that was much like fabric tearing, and dug their tin coffee cups out of the iced-shut pockets. When she got back to the propane stove, the water was on the cusp of boiling. "Come on, come on!" she grumbled at the pan.

When the first fat bubbles appeared at the surface of the water, Tessa took the paper sack out of the baggie and dropped a fistful of sugar into the pan. She jiggled the handle of the pan and then added another handful—and then another. She used a thick stick that had fallen off Randall's haul of firewood to stir the mixture. She tasted the liquid from the stick, grimaced at the thick sweetness, and poured it into the two cups.

Jessie motioned Tessa inside the tent but cautioned her, "They're doing fine, but they don't look real good. Don't react to them, Tess—they're gonna be fine."

R. E. and Kalluk were side by side in the middle of the small tent floor, each zippered into a sleeping bag, with only their heads visible. Tessa couldn't help her gasp. Their faces were a pasty, ashen white, and their teeth chattered so crazily that their entire faces trembled. The sharp clicking of their teeth banging together was louder than Tessa thought such a sound could ever be, outside of a nightmare. The sleeping bags twitched spastically from the uncontrollable shudders and shivers of their bodies.

Jessie took one of the cups from Tessa. "The chattering and shivers are good stuff, Tessa. Their bodies are trying to restore some heat through the motions." She moved to R. E.'s side, elevated his head with one hand, and brought the cup to his quivering lips. "Sip at it, R. E.," she said quietly. "I know it tastes awful, but you're going to drink this whole cup, so let's get going on it." She turned her head briefly to Tessa. "Look to Kalluk," she said. "Small sips is the way to go."

Tessa knelt at Kalluk's side and held the cup in her right hand. She reached for the back of his head and reflexively drew her hand back at the clammy coldness of his hair, scalp, and neck. *It's like touching a corpse.* She took a breath and again touched the back of Kalluk's head, lifting it a few inches. She touched the cup to his lips.

"Drink, Kalluk," she said. Then, she added, "Jessie'll get after you if you don't. She's already writing out a bill for her snowmobile."

Jessie snorted. "Darn straight," she said. "Those things don't float worth a darn, boys. See, that's why they call them snowmobiles, not water mobiles."

Kalluk's eyes found Tessa's, and through his pain she saw

a glint of light. His quaking mouth formed what could have been a smile. His lips moved as if he were trying to speak.

Tessa leaned closer to him. "I . . . what, Kalluk? Never mind—drink, don't try to talk." She tipped the cup to his mouth, but this time he moved his head weakly, negatively, and once again he struggled to form words. She leaned yet more forward over him, her ear close to his mouth. Kalluk raised his head another painful inch, kissed her cheek, and croaked, "Gotcha."

It was a bizarre moment. The humor—or whatever it was—was so very strange, so out of place, that it stunned her. Tessa sat back on her heels, shocked, spilling hot sugar water on Kalluk's throat. He grunted, but that labored smile appeared again on his face and in his eyes.

9

It was fully dark before Jessie allowed R. E. and Kalluk to leave their sleeping bags and the tent to sit at the fire with the others. The night was bitingly cold, with stars that were handfuls of precisely faceted diamonds flung on indigo velvet. There was no wind. The hiss and the crackle of the campfire seemed to be the only sound—at least until there was a sharp *crack* from the distant woods.

Tessa looked over that way, into the darkness. "What was that?"

"Branch cracking off a tree," Jessie answered. "I haven't seen it this cold in a long time. Some of the branches out there aren't thick enough to protect the sap. The sap freezes, expands, and the wood fractures." She gazed into the fire. "We're going to be hearing a lot more of that unless it warms up a little."

Kalluk and R. E. had filled their coffee cups and settled on the log with Jessie and Tessa. The brothers, on the far side of the fire, sat silently.

"What'd we lose, Kalluk?" Jessie asked, her voice neutral

and studiously non-accusatory. In spite of that, Kalluk's response was a bit defensive.

"I should have seen it, but I didn't. The weak spot must have been right above the spring feed. That water was moving fast—that's why it didn't freeze like the rest of it. I don't think anyone could have seen it."

Neither Tessa nor Jessie mentioned that Jessie had seen the fault and had tried to warn Kalluk away from it.

"Yeah. Maybe so," Jessie said. "What'd we lose?"

Kalluk shook his head. "Lots of stuff. The GPS. Clothes. My grill. A bunch of MREs. Our salt. A block of waterproof matches. Fishing line and hooks. Extra gloves, boots, a thermal blanket, chocolate—things like that."

"Nothing we can't live without," Jessie said. "We'll triangulate with our compasses, make a map, show landmarks. We'll find the sleds. I don't see that the MREs are a huge loss. Albin and Randall can keep us supplied with small game." She sighed. "I'll sure miss that chocolate, though."

"Like you said," R. E. said. "Nothing we can't live without, right? Anyway, I needed a bath."

Kalluk grinned sheepishly, looking for humor in a situation in which there was very little—or none. "It was kind of refreshing," he said. "Gets the ol' heart pumping."

"Next time we can have a little picnic before we go swimming," Jessie said.

"Ain't going to be a next time," Kalluk said, his voice now grim.

"You got that right, son," Jessie agreed. She stood. "Might as well get some sleep. We can stash the sleds tomorrow and start hoofin' it. You boys are lucky, R. E.—we brought sleeping bags for the brothers, and they won't use them. We'll—"

Tessa spoke before she could control her thought. "You mean we're going on? After this?"

The group was dead silent except for what might have been a chuckle from Randall or Albin on the other side of the fire.

Jessie stared at her. "'Course we're going on, Tess. Things happen out here. This wasn't more than a minor setback. Every trip has one. We just got ours outta the way earlier than most."

Fuzz settled himself on the other side of the tent fabric, his shoulder creating a small oblong indentation at Tessa's eye level. She braved a hand and arm outside her sleeping bag and scratched at the lump. Fuzz grunted in pleasure.

What a day! I thought those guys were lost for good. When Kalluk's head appeared—and then R. E.'s and Fuzz's—it was the most wonderful thing I've ever seen in my life. Thank you, God! Tessa pulled the sleeping bag flap more closely against the side of her head, as if she could shut out a thought. Her blunder of a comment about turning back nagged at her like a toothache. *The looks on their faces—and one of the brothers laughed at how silly what I said was—and those two* never *laugh.* She remembered one of Jessie's early comments long before the trip was under way. "This won't be a Girl Scout campout, Tess. It gets tough out there."

Yeah. It sure does. I saw some of that today. And what about Kalluk and his trick in the tent? What was that all about? He's the last person on earth I'd expect to pull something like that. Tessa squirmed in her sleeping bag and inadvertently nudged Fuzz through the fabric. He grunted in protest.

151

Come on, she told herself. *Get over it. You're acting crazy. Kalluk was probably half in shock and didn't know what he was doing.*

Another disquieting thought intruded. *Or did he know exactly what he was doing?*

❖◦❖◦❖

Jessie and Kalluk placed the three snowmobiles next to a prominent boulder and used their compasses to triangulate the position of the machines and the rock, using a small rise and a stand of trees as reference points. Each of them drew a sketch of the location and tucked the drawing away in an innermost pocket. "We'll find 'em on the way back," Jessie assured the group. "No doubt about it. Come on, let's saddle up. We're burnin' time."

The first full day of walking wasn't quite as difficult as Tessa had thought it would be. Albin and Randall hauled the two trailers. The boxes on runners slid almost effortlessly over the snow, providing very little drag, and pulling them along seemed to be no problem except on downgrades, where the front of the trailer tended to bang into the puller's heels. The brothers quickly solved that problem; they let the trailers lead and followed behind them, keeping them on the correct course with the pull ropes.

The brothers established and maintained a pace that was too fast and too tiring for all-day travel. Jessie, after shouting at Albin and Randall to slow it down a half dozen times, decided to let them go on ahead, but got their word they'd keep the others in sight. That worked out just fine. Even Kalluk seemed more comfortable at the slower walk. "Like

Jessie said," he told them, "you people can't be sucking down air this cold."

"And you can?" Jessie grumped. Kalluk pretended not to hear her.

Tessa and R. E. exchanged a rapid glance. Both had noticed that there was a bit of conflict between Jessie and Kalluk as to who was in charge of the expedition and who was giving the orders. "Too many generals and not enough privates," R. E. said quietly.

"Maybe so," Tessa answered. "But they both know what they're doing, so it doesn't make much difference."

"Yeah," R. E. said, again quietly. "And no matter what might happen, Albin and Randall would get us out of it."

It was a Fairbanks tourist-shop postcard sort of day. The color of the sky was a hue Tessa remembered from her days with Crayola crayons—sky blue. It was so deep and so unmarked by cloud cover of any kind that it looked almost artificial, like the overstated blue sky on a travel poster. The sun was bright, cheerful, and reflected glitteringly from the vast expanse of snow, making the group squint even behind their sunglasses. It looked like an August sun—but that's where the similarity ended. The temperature, according to Jessie and the thermocouple thermometer she carried, varied between minus twenty-five and minus twenty during full daylight. "It'll drop some at night," Kalluk observed.

Tessa and R. E. walked side by side, Jessie ahead of them by several feet, and Kalluk in front of her by a few feet. There'd been no real regimentation after the brothers were sent ahead; the walkers settled into their paces without strain. The surface of the snow was powdery, but there was relatively firm underfooting.

"I keep thinking about lunch," R. E. admitted.

"Me too. You wouldn't think we'd be so hungry just walking along," Tessa said. "I'm starved."

"The temperature's got a lot to do with it. When it's this cold, it takes lots of burning calories to maintain body heat." He grinned. "That's something I learned about yesterday."

"You're pretty perky for a guy who turned into a huge icicle and scared me half to death."

"To be honest, I hardly remember it. I recall going through the ice, but after that it's sort of a fog. I know we were in a tent, and I remember Jessie giving me sugar water, but that's about it until later in the evening. I seem to remember being underwater and how strong the current was and . . . and all that . . . but that's kind of dreamlike."

They walked on, boots squeaking on the snow in a monotonous but not unpleasant rhythm. "You were scared for me, huh?" R. E. asked.

"Of course I was. For you and Kalluk and Fuzz. It was a few awful moments until you all popped up."

"Well, it was one way to get your attention, Tess." There was a half-joking, half-serious shade to R. E.'s words.

"Come on, you don't need to crash into freezing water to get my attention." She smiled at him. They took several more steps before he spoke again.

"How about this: if I sit on the edge of a hole and just dangle my feet in to get your attention, is that OK?"

Tessa laughed, and when she drew in a breath, her throat burned. "That'll be fine," she gasped. "Don't make me laugh anymore. It hurts too much."

The lunch stop came relatively late. Light was beginning to fade when Kalluk raised his arm to signal a stop. The brothers, now not much larger than dots on the horizon, swung back toward the rest of the group.

"How'd they know we're stopping?" Tessa asked Jessie.

Jessie shook her head. "Beats me. But I'll tell you what: those boys don't miss a thing out here, no matter what it is. Maybe one of them looks back every few steps. Or maybe it's intuition or something. I've seen the same sort of thing in other Inuits."

Tessa waved at Albin and Randall. When neither returned the wave she felt foolish. "They do things differently than we do, Tess. No wasted motion," Jessie said. "They weren't snubbing you," she added. "Actually, they like you, which is saying a lot for those two."

The propane stove brought the coffee to a boil and heated MREs two at a time. Fuzz had found his own lunch, Tessa noticed. His muzzle was spattered with blood, and bits of fur adhered to his chest and neck. The stop lasted barely a half hour. As the brothers started out, Kalluk caught them, and the three men spoke for a moment. Then, the brothers went on at their usual unwavering pace and speed.

Kalluk again took the lead. The walking became, as it had earlier, an automatic process, one that involved little strain and no thought. It was a matter of taking a step and then following it with another. Jessie and Kalluk had early on discussed equipping the group with snowshoes and had then decided against it. Almost all of the territory they'd cover was open and windswept, and the base of snow had hardened to a concrete-like surface under a scant few inches of new snow. The towering trees in the wooded areas they encountered acted as umbrellas keeping most of the snow from ever reaching the forest floor.

155

The abbreviated daylight hours made for a short day of walking. When Kalluk waved to the brothers, R. E. and Tessa sank gratefully to the snow. "For a five-hour day," R. E. commented, "it sure seemed a lot longer."

"We covered some ground today, though," Tessa said. "We'll get used to the walking. But you're right—I was ready to pack it in for the day."

Jessie selected a campsite under a stand of a dozen or so pines, and the group began foraging for firewood. Tessa flinched as a gunshot boomed across the tundra, rudely disturbing the peace. Kalluk grinned. "No MREs tonight," he said. "We'll have fresh meat of some kind."

"One shot?" R. E. asked.

Jessie and Kalluk looked at him as if he'd asked if ice was cold. "Those boys haven't wasted a bullet since they were in diapers," Jessie said. "We'll have meat."

Jessie was right. Albin and Randall pulled the trailers into camp with one loaded with firewood and the other with a large goose draped over it. Albin took it aside to clean it. Tessa averted her gaze. Plucking the goose would have required more time and a great deal of boiling water, so Albin skinned it instead. Fuzz danced around Albin, waiting for the assorted treats he knew would be coming his way.

The meal was splendid; even Tessa had to agree with that point. She settled into her sleeping bag later, her eyes already too heavy to keep open from the fine meal and the weariness from the day's walk.

She woke only once during the night, startled awake by the cracking of a tree limb. The familiar lump in the tent's fabric was at her side.

10

The next few days of walking followed in a monotonous chain of seeing the same things, doing the same things, and eating the same things. The sighting of an eagle gliding on the thermals far above the snow was no longer an event that elicited comment; it wasn't that the smooth, majestic grace of the bird was less than breathtakingly beautiful—it was a matter of repetition of the same scene. Jessie and Kalluk, in fact, had seen eagles all their lives and didn't find them to be remarkable. The brothers felt much the same. "Always there," Albin had said when Tessa called his attention to the sky and a swooping eagle.

Jessie and Kalluk didn't converse a great deal, but R. E. and Tessa found that the time—and the miles—passed easier when they were engaged in conversation. When they'd exhausted the topics that came to mind, they played a word definition game with spontaneously generated rules.

"Define the word *onomatopoeia*," Tessa said.

"I know this one . . . gimme a minute . . ."

Tessa began loudly humming the *Jeopardy!* theme song.

"It's . . . ahhh . . . the . . . it's the sound of a word that kinda *is* the word, isn't it?"

Tessa finished the music. "That's not a complete answer. Sorry."

"Come on, Tess! It refers to a . . . well . . . a sound that's kind of reproduced in a word. *Whoosh* is one. *Pow* is another. See what I mean?"

"'See what I mean' isn't a valid answer, and you still owe me points for the last word you missed."

Every so often Jessie would look back over her shoulder, as if wondering what the laughter was about. After listening to the game for a bit, she hurried her pace to put more distance between herself and R. E. and Tessa.

When they'd worn out the game, they walked in silence, comfortable with the quiet. Tessa no longer flinched at the sound of a tree limb freezing and breaking; when they were near wooded areas, the high-pitched snapping sounds were quite frequent.

"There's nowhere else I'd rather be," R. E. said after a few minutes.

"I know what you mean. I never realized how beautiful Alaska is, and I've seen a ton of travel programs and magazine layouts and all that. There's something here that no television show or video disc can convey."

"Alaska-itis," R. E. said. "It's an inflammation of the heart, I think. The only cure is to live here."

That comment might have drawn a chuckle from Tessa, but the tone of R. E.'s voice precluded that. He seemed serious; there was no silliness to the words. It was simply an affirmation of a truth in R. E.'s mind.

"That's a sweet way to put it," Tessa said.

After a few more steps, R. E. asked, "How does it compare to Minnesota?"

"Hard to say. There's a whole lot I like here, but Minnesota is home. It's funny. I've only been here a short time, but already my memories of home and the university are kind of fuzzy around the edges. That's not the fault of the school or my home state—it's that everything here is so enchanting. Maybe I'd get used to seeing an eagle swooping around like the brothers have." After a moment, she added, "But I doubt it."

"You could stay, you know." R. E. stopped walking.

So did Tessa. She turned to him. "All this is temporary for me, R. E."

They began walking again. "Maybe you'll find a reason to stay," R. E. said.

Throughout the morning and into the afternoon Fuzz alternated between hanging a dozen or so feet behind Tessa and walking in the heel position with Kalluk. The wolf-dog seemed to be having a grand time. Gulping the dangerously frigid air had no effect on him. When he'd break away from the party to follow a scent, he'd often return with an offering for Tessa: half of a ptarmigan, the hindquarters of a rabbit, or some other culinary delight. The fact that Tessa never touched Fuzz's offerings offended him not in the least.

"It's the thought that counts," R. E. observed as he poked a bloody midsection of a small animal with the toe of his boot.

"Sure." Tessa laughed. "By the way, I have something for you."

"For me? What? Why?"

"Don't you know what today is?"

"I . . . sure. Tuesday, isn't it? Or Wednesday?"

"It's Christmas, R. E." She unbuttoned her coat, tugged a mitten off with her teeth, and reached inside the layers of her shirts and sweaters. She pulled out a small rectangular package wrapped in Christmas paper with a crumpled red bow. "Merry Christmas," she said, holding the package out to R. E.

"I'd completely forgotten about Christmas," R. E. said. "I have a really nice Christmas gift for you back home, Tessa, but I didn't want to bring it along and take up space needed for supplies. I'm really sorry."

"There's nothing to be sorry about. Go on, open your present."

R. E. pulled his gloves off, stuffed them in his coat pocket, and went to work on the ribbon. After fiddling with it for a full minute, he gave up and simply broke it. Then, he pulled away the paper. A pair of king-size Hershey bars—with almonds—looked back at him through the torn wrapping paper. He smiled. "These are great, Tess. With almonds too—my favorite. This was wonderful of you—a real surprise. I thought all the chocolate was packed away in the trailer when Kalluk and I went into the water."

"Those bars rode in my backpack all this time, waiting for today." She paused for a moment. "I know what you mean about forgetting about what day this is. Everything's different out here—as if individual days don't matter, and only the distance covered counts. It's strange, in a way. It must be the way the People feel as they move with the seasons."

"Probably so. I don't imagine they have much use for calendars."

"I know what you mean."

160

"Hey, about Christmas—we'll do it up right when we get home, OK? We'll cut a tree and make a big meal and sing carols and all that."

Tessa wasn't at all sure what she was hearing in R. E.'s voice. His words were a little rapid—he was excited—but there was a texture of . . . of what? It was as if he were asking her permission to do something, to get her approval on whatever it was he had in mind.

"Sure," she finally said. "We can have the others there too. That'll be fun. And I just might have a little gift at my place for you, R. E. It might even be all wrapped and have a red ribbon that doesn't look like it's been banged around for two weeks."

R. E. smiled and moved to her for a quick hug. She glanced over his shoulder as he embraced her. Kalluk had stopped and turned and was watching them. She stiffened, and R. E. stepped back as if he'd gotten an electric shock.

"What's the matter?" he asked.

"Nothing—I got a chill, is all. Let's get moving again. It's not good to stand around in this cold."

R. E. looked at her rather dubiously. "OK," he finally said. "Let's go. Wanna play some more of our word game?"

"No, not really. Not just now." She softened her refusal with a gentle "OK?"

What was that all about? Tessa wondered, suddenly irked at herself. *There's no reason in the world I should feel guilty about giving R. E. an innocent hug. And where does Kalluk get off gawking at me like a father watching his teen daughter kissing her boyfriend on the front porch?*

When Kalluk signaled for a stop and waved Albin and Randall in, Tessa was ready to end the day—not because

161

of physical weariness but because of a desire to escape the thoughts that were nagging at her.

⊷•⊷•⊶

They made camp fifty yards into a forest and used the natural shelter the trees provided. There was ample dead-wood and enough light left to easily find it. As Tessa hauled an armload to the pile she noticed Jessie standing off to the side, looking down at the pocket thermometer held in her gloved hand. Jessie shook her head briefly and put the thermometer back in her pocket. When she noticed Tessa looking at her she offered an obviously forced smile.

What's that about? Tessa wondered. She started toward Jessie, but the woman turned away and walked to Kalluk, who was pulling MREs out of a trailer. Kalluk, crouched, looked up at his friend. Jessie leaned close, and they exchanged a few words. Kalluk shook his head slightly, repeating the almost unconscious movement of Jessie a few moments earlier. Tessa dropped her armful of wood next to the brothers, who were creating one of their perfectly symmetrical, pyramidal stacks. She glanced again toward Kalluk and Jessie. They'd already separated, and Jessie was checking the tautness of the tents. *Strange,* Tessa thought. *I wonder what's going on?*

R. E., a rope over his shoulder, skidded a four foot long, foot and a half wide log over the snow to the side of the piled wood. "Our easy chair for the night," he said. "Got another coming too." The second log was shorter but equally thick. Butted together, they made a continuous six-foot-long seating arrangement that gave Kalluk, Jessie, R. E., and Tessa plenty of room for sitting to eat, drink coffee, and talk after the meal. Albin and Randall, as usual, hunkered down on

162

the other side of the fire, uninvolved in conversation with the others. Fuzz ranged about the camp, stopping occasionally to raise his snout to catalog a scent and then moving on. The wolf-dog seemed skittish—his tail was tucked a bit more deeply between his hind legs than usual. When a nearby branch cracked, Fuzz jerked as if he'd been struck by a lash. He scrambled back from the sound, his fangs glinting in the early moonlight, before he spun and ran into the darker woods.

Tessa stood watching until the wolf-dog disappeared. She moved over to Jessie.

"What's up?" she asked. "I saw you checking your thermometer earlier and then talking to Kalluk."

"Nothing new. I check it a few times a day."

Tessa met Jessie's eyes. "How cold is it, Jessie?"

"Very. We're going to talk about it after we eat. Let's let it go until then."

"Is there something wrong?"

Jessie sighed. "We've maybe got to take a few more precautions. We'll talk about it—see what the brothers think, what Kalluk thinks. Don't worry about it. We know what we're doing." Jessie looked away, quite obviously ending the conversation. She sniffed the still air. "That coffee smells great, doesn't it?"

The evening meal was good, particularly the dessert, which was an apple crumb sort of cake that wasn't half bad. The MREs, meat loaf with brown gravy, were a bit cardboardy, but hot and filling, which compensated for their bland flavor. The coffee was, as ever, excellent.

Kalluk, mug in hand, stood and waved Albin and Randall over to where he, R. E., Jessie, and Tessa were sitting close to the fire. The brothers stood just within the firelight, looking like a pair of shaggy bookends.

"It seems like we have some weather coming," Kalluk began. "Of course, we lost the weather radio in the water. Jessie says the temp is very low—over fifty below zero. That's bad enough when things are as still as they are now, but with storm winds, it'd be downright deadly. So, we've got a choice to make."

Jessie stood and moved next to Kalluk. "It's my feeling that we're in a decent place here. I want to hole up, gather all the wood we can, maybe go a little deeper into the forest, and wait this thing out."

R. E. raised his hand like a schoolboy. Jessie nodded at him.

"Are you sure there's a storm coming? The sky has been clear, and there's no wind, just like Kalluk said. I want to do the safe thing, but I'm worried about meeting up with Kalluk's People too."

One of the brothers—it was hard to say which since their faces were in shadows from the fire—said, "It comes."

"Yeah," Jessie agreed. "It's coming. The question is when it'll hit." She directed her words to R. E. and Tessa. "If it were just me or Kalluk picking up on the signs, maybe I'd be less sure. But I've never known Albin and Randall to be wrong about this sort of thing. They're more accurate than any weather radio."

"Kalluk," Tessa asked, "what do you want us to do?"

"Check the weather—the temp and the wind, the sky configuration—through the night. Actually, the temperature doesn't mean that much if we take precautions. If things look OK, we move on at first light, just as we've been doing.

First sign of a storm, we hole up, but we'll have covered some ground. Like R. E. pointed out, we have a date with some of the People, and they're not going to hang around waiting for us."

Jessie took a step away from Kalluk, as if the distance would make their arguments more distinct. "I've run a whole lot of trips out here," she said. "I've lost only one person, and he had a heart attack that no one could have possibly predicted."

"Jessie—" Kalluk began, but she motioned him into silence with a quick downward motion.

"I know there's something coming," she said calmly. "I don't know for sure what it is. It may be over in a few hours. Or, maybe not." She looked directly at Kalluk. "I think we gotta set up here. There's no doubt in my mind. If we don't, we'll be endangering the—"

"How about a vote, then, excluding Tessa and R. E.?" Kalluk interrupted. His eyes went to Tessa's. "No disrespect, but we . . ."

"No problem," Tessa said. R. E. agreed.

"OK. Good," Kalluk said. He turned to face the brothers. "What do you boys think?"

"We watch but go," Albin said.

"Randall?"

"What Albin said."

Kalluk shifted his gaze to Jessie.

"I say we move into the woods and hole up right now," she said.

Kalluk nodded. "I say we go—that we keep a close watch all night, but that we move on in the morning if we can."

"That's it, then," Jessie said, her voice level. "Maybe we

165

ought to turn in. If we go tomorrow, we want to get started as early as possible."

They loaded wood into the fire with little conversation. Tessa was tired, but she didn't yet head for her sleeping bag. Albin and Randall went outside the light of the fire, and R. E. was already in his and Kalluk's tent. Jessie and Kalluk sat on the seating log, finishing the dregs that remained in the coffeepot and talking quietly. Tessa joined them just as Jessie rose and tossed grounds from her cup into the flames. "I'm gonna turn in," she said.

"'Night," Kalluk said. "We'll see what happens tomorrow."

"Right."

"I'll be along in a few minutes," Tessa said. "Good night, Jessie."

Tessa sat on the log and hefted the coffeepot. "Still a drop or so left," she said. She took her cup from her pocket and poured an inch of very dark-looking coffee into it.

"We haven't really talked since R. E. and I went swimming," Kalluk said. "That kissing thing—I was . . . I dunno. You looked so scared, Tessa, and I couldn't talk much, and I just wanted to let you know I was OK."

Tessa sipped her coffee, grimaced, said, "Yuck," and tossed it into the fire. "It's no big deal. Let's forget about it."

"I don't want to do that. What I'd like is for us—some day soon—to kiss like it really means something."

"Kalluk . . ."

"No, please. Just listen to me for a minute. I'm no good at this kind of stuff. What I meant was that you've impressed me. We have a lot in common, and I like that."

Tessa was momentarily flustered. "Kalluk, this is insane!

166

We hardly even know each other, and you're coming out with this stuff?"

"Things are different with my people."

"But that's just it; I'm not one of your people. Let's just go to our tents and forget that this conversation ever—"

"The People don't go through all the elaborate nonsense lower 48ers do, Tessa. We let our feelings be known. I'm of the People, and I act as they act." He stood at the same time Tessa did, and held her in place with his eyes. That bizarre dizzy sensation touched her once again. Kalluk, after a century or so, broke eye contact. "Good night, Tessa," he said as he turned away and headed toward the tent he shared with R. E. Tessa didn't answer. Instead, she watched Kalluk's back for a moment and then walked slowly to her own tent.

Tessa snuggled into her sleeping bag and felt the slow embrace of the warmth her body generated. She'd grown accustomed to having Jessie sleep a foot or so away from her, and had come to see the woman's hushed, slightly sibilant breathing as a comfortable, calming type of white noise. Tonight, though, tranquility eluded her.

Jessie looked so grim when she was outvoted. She knows Alaska at least as well as Kalluk and maybe even as well as the brothers. Still, Albin and Randall are hunters and natives who've faced every sort of blizzard and storm imaginable, at least according to Meeloa. Jessie admits that too. Kalluk has been all over Alaska, living with the People, living as they have for centuries. It could be that Jessie is a little too conscious of the lower 48 tourists she's led for so many years. This trek is different, Tessa thought. *It's not a vacation or a photo shoot.*

Jessie said something in her sleep, the words too quiet and too slurred for Tessa to understand. *Probably just a bad dream. Like this craziness from Kalluk—his talk about showing his feelings was so strange. And the way the man's eyes make me feel* . . .

Tessa eased a hand and part of her arm from the sleeping bag to stroke the familiar lump of Fuzz sleeping outside. He wasn't there. *First time for that,* she thought as she surrendered to sleep. Later—much later—Fuzz settled down outside the tent, but he didn't sleep. After a few minutes he tested the air, rose, shook himself, and loped off deeper into the woods.

11

When Tessa was drawn out of her tent the next morning by the sound of voices and the smell of brewing coffee, the sky was a used-dishwater hue, a flat, featureless gray that allowed little sunlight to penetrate it. Jessie was poking at the coals of the night's fire with a stick and adding wood. She glanced up at Tessa. "Soon as you get some coffee in you, you'd better get the tents down and packed, Tess. We gotta get rollin'."

"Will do, Jessie." Tessa took her mess cup from her pocket and moved a few steps to join R. E., Kalluk, and the brothers. They were all staring up at the sky as if something very important had been written there by a giant hand. Tessa followed the men's eyes with her own. What she'd thought was a stagnant, motionless mass of low-hanging, dirty-gray clouds wasn't that at all. The sky was churning, roiling like a boiling cauldron, huge shrouds of gray being transformed into smaller, faster-moving vaporous bodies. "That's what the sky looks like just before a tornado," she said.

"Does Alaska get tornados?" R. E. asked.

"I've never seen one," Kalluk said. "Albin? Randall?"

"One maybe in our lives," Randall said. His brother nodded toward the sky. "Ain't no tornado."

Jessie had approached the group, her cup of coffee in hand. "No, it isn't," she said. "Coffee's ready, and the meals are on the coals. If we're going to go this morning, let's get to it. I say we stick close to the edge of the forest until this thing is over."

The brothers nodded.

"Yeah," Kalluk agreed. "Good point."

Breakfast was a rapid meal with none of the talk and banter that usually signaled the start of a day. The brothers were pulling the trailers and were checking the loads, making certain that everything was secure. Jessie and Tessa scraped snow over the coals of the fire and then stepped back from the wet steam that was produced.

The brothers set out first, as usual. Kalluk followed a short distance behind them, with Jessie behind him, and Tessa and R. E. behind Jessie by several feet. Albin and Randall stopped after they'd gone twenty-five yards and waved Kalluk to them. He jogged out. The men talked for a brief moment, all apparently looking at something in the snow, and then Kalluk jogged back.

"Wolf tracks," he said. "Maybe five or six of them. Kinda strange they'd come out in the open so close to us and our fire."

"Fuzz was skittish last night," Tessa said. "Maybe he heard or smelled them."

"Speaking of Fuzz," Kalluk said but didn't finish the sentence. Instead he tugged off a glove and raised his fingers to his mouth. The keening shriek seemed piercing enough to carry to California.

"Look," R. E. said as he pointed to the tree line. Fuzz was coming toward them, but he seemed like a different animal. He carried his body a full three inches lower than he normally did, and his tongue was like a pink flag at his mouth. Even at that distance it was easy to see that the wolf-dog's eyes were open much wider than usual. His grace of movement was altered; he moved jerkily, head darting from side to side, his gait stiff, his hackles raised the length of his back.

"Is he afraid of the wolves?" R. E. asked.

"No," Jessie said. "I doubt that he and the wolves would fight—Fuzz is bigger and stronger than most of the alpha males. He's feeling the storm, and he's scared. I've known him for most of his life, and I've never seen him slink like that before."

"Me neither," Kalluk grunted. He turned abruptly from Fuzz's approach. "Come on, let's get in gear." He waved to the brothers, and the trek began again. Tessa and R. E. were quiet as they constantly checked the sky and wondered what the next hour would bring.

"What do you think, Tess?" It wasn't necessary for R. E. to name what he was referring to.

"I don't think we should have left camp—we should have dug in and gotten ready. I don't know—maybe it's the way the sky looks, or Fuzz's fear, but I'm just plain scared now."

"Me too," R. E. said. "I keep telling myself that Kalluk and the brothers are old hands at this stuff, and that they know what they're doing. But, look at that sky—and we're losing light already, and it isn't even midday yet."

"There's no wind at all, though. Maybe the storm is kind of localized somewhere else. That could be, right?"

171

R. E. chuckled quietly. "You sound like you're asking me if the tooth fairy is real, and hoping I'll say yes."

"Mmmm. That's not too far off, I guess." Tessa took a few more steps before she turned away from R. E. and spat. The saliva wasn't more than a couple of inches from her mouth before it froze with a tiny snap. R. E. glanced at her quickly and then looked away, as if he'd caught her belching loudly at a funeral service.

"It's a test Jessie showed me," she explained. "A way to see how cold it is."

"Oh. How cold is it?"

"Too cold."

Tessa looked ahead beyond Jessie, where Kalluk walked, Fuzz at his heel. *He must know what he's doing. Albin and Randall wanted to go on too.* She watched Kalluk as he moved ahead at his smooth, regular pace. Then suddenly he stopped short, as if he'd heard his name, signaled a stop, and motioned the brothers back.

"'Bout time," Jessie said.

The group gathered around Kalluk. "We can't risk this any longer. I've never seen a sky like this. We gotta get ready for the storm."

All eyes moved to the brothers.

"Good," Albin said. Randall nodded.

Jessie pointed to the woods. "Our best bet is to get some cover between us and the weather. Let's do it."

Randall touched her arm. "Cave better, Jessie." He pointed back toward the path they'd covered. "We saw there by frozen stream."

"Go," Kalluk said.

172

"But," R. E. questioned, "there are bears around here, aren't there? Suppose there's one hibernating in there."

Albin caught R. E.'s glance and tapped the lump in his coat just above his belt line with the fingertips of his right hand.

"Oh," R. E. said.

This time they clustered behind the brothers rather than stringing out in their usual travel formation. To Tessa and R. E. the terrain was exactly the same in all directions, except for the periphery of the forest on one side and the occasional low hill.

It took them over an hour to backtrack, taking them past their last night's camp a mile or so. Tessa didn't realize that there was a cave until she was standing directly in front of it, watching Randall scooping and kicking away a drift of snow that partially covered its mouth.

The mouth was about four feet high and roughly oval in shape. The cave was pitch black, but Kalluk's six-cell Maglite pierced the darkness. The interior rose sharply immediately inside the mouth to a jagged ceiling perhaps eight feet from the floor. Jessie stepped next to Kalluk and took a disposable lighter from her pocket. She scratched it to a flame, and the orangish red tongue bent toward the rear of the cave. "Good," she said. "We got lucky. There's some draw. We'll be able to keep a fire going."

Kalluk shone his light deeper into the cave. The room they were in extended back about twenty feet, with the ceiling angling downward until, at the very rear, the opening was about a foot and a half. Tessa took a tentative step and felt her boot crunch on something. Kalluk swung his light to her feet. The long-dead remains of a fire—gray ash and small, mostly consumed pieces of wood—evidenced the fact that this party wasn't the cave's first human inhabitants.

"First thing we need to do is gather up all the wood we can find and get it in here," Kalluk said. His voice sounded deeper—even more Johnny Cash-ish because of the acoustics of the stone walls and ceiling. "There should be plenty—this is a fairly wide stream, and the spring runoff and flooding would have deposited good firewood at the banks and snagged it on rocks."

"Let's stay in couples, people," Jessie said. "We don't know when this thing is going to hit. How about Tess going with Albin, R. E. with Randall, and Kalluk and I will pair up. Let's not wander too far from the cave. We'll get wood and then drag the trailers in here and see what we can do about setting up. We could be here a couple of days."

"What about safety lines?" Kalluk asked.

"Not for now, I don't think. As long as we keep the mouth of the cave in sight, we'll be OK. Anchoring us to something here would slow us down. Just don't wander too far."

Tessa followed Albin out of the cave, crouching at the low mouth, duck-walking through, and then standing. By contrast with the inky blackness inside, the slug-gray overcast seemed almost cheerful. The sky, if anything, was actually darker, and seething maniacally. The wind remained perfectly still. It was a dead calm, a foreboding sort of breathless quiet.

"Spooky," she said. Albin didn't answer.

Jessie had been correct about the wood. Albin headed directly toward a series of several boulders, mounded over with snow. He began sweeping at the base of the rocks, revealing broken branches and some larger sections of tree trunks. Tessa rushed to help, shoving snow with her arms. "No," Albin said. She looked at him. "Don't work fast. Cold. Move slow." After a second, he added, "Tessa."

First time he's called me by name. Tessa reflected for a moment. *Actually, I think this is the first time he's spoken directly to me. I'm glad he reminded me, though—after a life of being a nonsmoker, I don't need to mess up my lungs.* She scraped at the snow more slowly, uncovered a long branch, and pulled it free. She set it aside and dug for more wood. The pile at Tessa's side grew rapidly as she uncovered limbs and branches that'd snagged against and between the boulders. She was crouching to wrap her arms around the heap when Kalluk's strident whistle slashed the silence. She stood back up. Fuzz broke from the tree line at a full, hard run, seeming to course over the snow, head low, body extended. At the same moment Tessa saw the wolf-dog, the cacophonous roar of a hundred out-of-control freight trains shattered the air and tore open the dull gray of the sky. It couldn't have logically been called a snowfall; instead it was an impenetrable, writhing, swirling wall of white—and it was moving faster than Fuzz was running. He seemed to know that, and it made his flight somehow pathetic, a tragic drama that could not possibly end well.

Tessa watched, horror struck, her precious wood forgotten, as the white mass touched Fuzz and flung his back end and rear legs up and forward and slammed him, inverted, onto his back twenty feet ahead. He scrambled to get up, all of his paws seeking purchase. He was close enough now to Tessa and Albin that the red-pink of his tongue and the fear in his eyes showed clearly. Then the storm swallowed him, sweeping over where he'd fallen, enveloping him as if he were a speck of dust in a hurricane.

Tessa wasn't certain that she was screaming. Her throat felt the sensation of a scream, but there was no way any human sound could penetrate the screech of the wind. She'd taken a step toward where she'd last seen Fuzz when Albin tackled her, ramming her down into the snow and pinning her body to the ground with his own weight, his hooded head and shaggy hair next to her face. "Stay!" he hollered into her ear. "Can't run now. We stay, then we run."

The streambed was an indentation from the flatland around it, its bottom perhaps three feet below level, cutting a twisting course over years of spring runoff and summer rainstorms. In another fifty years it might be ten or even twenty feet deep, or it could simply stay as it was now if the rushing waters were diverted by a quirk of nature in another direction. This day it was a lifesaver. The leading edge of the blizzard winds raked across the plain and into the forest, uprooting trees, shearing others, bludgeoning standing trees with those wrenched from the frozen ground.

The earth trembled under the power of the storm. Albin's weight pressed Tessa's body against the snow and rocks of the streambed. The din was beyond human comprehension—the roar of the wrath of nature unleashed, proving how very feeble man and his inventions really were.

Even with her layered clothing and with Albin's mass on top of her, the minus fifty degree temperature began to tease Tessa's mind, to lead her to the darkness. Her thoughts became disjointed, her perceptions askew. Strangely, she wasn't shivering although she was profoundly chilled. *It's getting warmer—it really is. And I'm so tired. Funny—it's too early in the day to be so tired. We haven't gone far. The storm is almost over. I can barely hear it now. A warm front must be*

*following it, 'cause I'm so much warmer. This is like sliding down
a long, smooth, velvet slope and into a big four-poster bed piled
with quilts and comforters and blankets.*

"Time for cave." The words came from a distance, and
Tessa couldn't place the voice. It was somehow familiar, but
no face came to mind.

"Tessa. Now."

Tessa realized that she was being shaken by the shoulders,
and the rest of reality filtered painfully back. The storm
howled on, but the voice of its roar was no longer steady; it
was higher pitched with peaks of sound followed by equally
strident valleys.

"You hold my coat with two hands and don't let go."
Albin's face was inches from hers, and she knew there must
be some warmth in his breath, but she could feel none.
"My face is numb," she mumbled through lips that wouldn't
move. Albin either didn't hear her or wasn't interested in
the numbness of her face at the moment. "You can hold," he
said. "I carry some wood. You hold. Don't let go." The wind
screamed. An image of Fuzz being catapulted through the
air by the storm flickered in Tessa's mind. She swallowed
and nodded.

Albin released Tessa's shoulders and held a gloved finger
in front of her face. "Minute," he said and turned away. He
was lost to her in a blinding whirlpool of snow before he'd
taken a second step. She wobbled on her benumbed feet
as the wind buffeted her, forcing her one way and then
immediately another. She held her right arm out straight
ahead of her, squinting at it. She couldn't see beyond her
elbow. That frightened her more than anything else about
the storm had. A gust from behind her shoved her ahead

a few stumbling, disoriented steps. She went down on one knee, started to rise, and was slammed back down by another blast of wind. She had no idea what distance she'd lurched from where Albin had left her. *Feet? Yards? Even if I scream he won't be able to hear me. What if . . .*

Tessa had never been so glad to feel the touch of another human being as she was at the insistent nudge of Albin's hand at her shoulder. He stepped in front of her, his arms loaded with firewood that reached to his nose. Tessa locked her hands into the shaggy elk hide his coat was fashioned from. Even with next to no sensation in her hands or fingers, this was a grip she knew she'd never loosen until she was safe or there was no more life in her. As she lumbered after Albin, her clenched hands occasionally bumped against his back. Although his coat was thick and his clothing underneath layered, it felt as if she had come in contact with a solid wall; there was no more slack in his muscles than there was in a piece of marble. *He'll get me through,* she thought. *All I need to do is follow him.*

The trek took either fifteen minutes or several eternities. Tessa wasn't sure which. How Albin could see where he was going, Tessa had no idea; she'd long since closed her eyes and shambled after the man she was connected to by her hands, as trusting of him as a newborn infant clutching her mother.

When Albin stopped and then crouched, Tessa thought he had fallen. She bent over him as he turned his face back to her and hollered over the wind, "Cave." Her hands refused to release Albin's coat, and he dragged her inside, loaded down with more wood than a single man should have to carry under such conditions.

At first the fire in the cave appeared to Tessa as a shimmering orange glow. Then, as R. E. was prying her fingers away from the fur of Albin's coat, images became more distinct. Jessie sat on one of the trailers, guiding MREs into the fire with a stick. Kalluk stood next to her. The coffeepot was balanced on three rocks arranged as a triangle to the side of the fire, its bottom a few inches above the flames. Her fingers suddenly radiated pain, the muscles screaming at her as she released the death-grip clutch she'd been demanding from them.

"You're OK now," Jessie murmured, embracing her. "We're all here and we're all safe, and that's what counts. Let's get you over to the fire and thaw you out."

Albin stomped snow from his boots on the stone floor of the cave, dumped his load of wood, and faced the fire for a few moments. Then he strode over to where Randall was hunkered down.

Tessa's teeth were beginning to chatter, and her body shook with uncontrollable shivering. "Albin," she called through cold-stiffened lips, "thanks. Thank you."

Albin turned to her and nodded.

Bringing Tessa's body back to a near-normal temperature was a painful process. As the fire warmed her, nerves cried out as sensation returned. Her feet alternated between what felt like scalding heat, numbness, and a return to their frigid state. She sat on the log close to the fire, huddled under blankets. She shook half the coffee out of the mug R. E. handed to her; the refills became small splashes that would stay within the mug. Jessie stood behind Tess, working her shoulders and back muscles, her thumbs pressing and kneading. "R. E. wanted to go out after you," Jessie said. "Kalluk and I had to hold him back. We knew that if anyone could get you to the cave, it was Albin. We—Kalluk and me—were just getting back with wood. We managed to get one of the trailers inside, but the other took off like a big, tall bird in that first blast of wind. We lost some stuff we need."

"How bad off are we?" Tessa asked.

Jessie waited for a moment before answering. "We can make it through the storm. I'm pretty sure of that, unless it goes on for longer than any storm I've ever experienced. After that, the brothers can feed us with game. We've got the tents at least, but the medical kit, most of the MREs, canned goods, hand tools—the hand axes and the long one—are gone."

Tessa slurped coffee and swallowed, waiting for Jessie to continue. When Jessie didn't speak, Tessa did. "Can we go on?"

Jessie shook her head sadly. "I don't think so. We've lost too many essentials. It'd be too dangerous. I'll talk to Kalluk, but I don't think . . ."

Kalluk approached from behind Jessie. "We might just as well talk now, Jessie," he said. "Randall, Albin, c'mon over here for a minute, will you?" The brothers walked over together and stood facing Kalluk. R. E. sat next to Tessa on the log. Jessie remained standing, still massaging Tessa's back. Kalluk stepped in front of the fire.

He sighed before he spoke. "We—I—lost a sled. I lost a trailer. I lost Fuzz. Some very important things were on the trailer that blew away today. I don't see any options or alternatives, folks. We need to start back to the snowmobiles as soon as the storm lets up." Kalluk looked directly at Tessa. "I'm sorry, Tessa and R. E. I know this trip was important to you." He shifted his gaze to the brothers. "I'll see that you boys are paid for the entire trip. I know that you two would go on, and that you'd make it to the end—if you were alone. That's not the case."

Neither brother spoke.

"Comments, anyone?" Kalluk asked.

"It's the only decision we could make, Kalluk," Jessie said. "We couldn't—"

The branches and limbs that'd been piled in front of the opening at the front of the cave exploded inward, and snow, ice, and wood erupted as if struck by a cannonball.

Fuzz, snow covered, tongue hanging from the side of his mouth, skidded to a stop in front of Kalluk. Kalluk embraced the wolf-dog as he would a long-lost best friend.

Tessa was the first one to begin clapping, even though she could barely feel her hands. R. E. and Jessie joined in, and after a moment, so did Randall and Albin. Now, at least they were all together. No lives had been lost.

Thank you, Lord.

12

Mugs of coffee, the blankets, and the fire—which was kept high in order to dispel the dampness of the cave—brought Tessa's normal sensations slowly back to her. Fuzz, after his frantically joyful greeting of Kalluk, had settled next to Tessa, soaking up the heat just as she was.

Jessie heated and passed out MREs with the announcement, "This is gonna be it for grub today, so enjoy it. We've got to conserve; we don't know how long we'll be here or how long it'll take us to get to the sleds."

"Don't matter," Albin said. "Plenty of game."

"I'm not so sure about that," Jessie said. "Even you boys'd have a tough time finding anything in this storm—and if you did, there's no guarantee you'd make it back to the cave."

The brothers grinned at one another, but neither replied.

The storm rolled on, unabated, through the balance of the day. If anything, the wind seemed to gain power as the hours dragged by. Tessa huddled as close to the fire as she could get without bursting into flame. Heat, she decided, was something she'd never, ever take for granted again. The eerie, moaning, hollow sound the gusts produced as they howled past the mouth of the cave reminded her of a five-day anthropology conference she'd attended in New York City three years ago. The hotel room the university had paid for was nice enough, but the constant sound of traffic—blaring horns, squealing tires, grinding metal-against-metal brakes—was constantly outside her window.

"I don't know how native New Yorkers do it," she'd said to an anthro professor from Chicago. "This racket would drive me nuts, and I'd probably never sleep at all."

He'd looked at her blankly. "What racket? There's lots of construction, but none of it is close to the hotel."

"The cars, the horns—all that."

"You'll get used to it. In a couple of days you won't even notice it."

She smiled to herself now as she stared into the fire.

The guy from Chicago was right. A day or so later, unless I stopped to really think about it, the noise had simply become a part of where I was, not much different from the throngs of scurrying people, the impossibly tall buildings, the hustling, racing pace of life. It's like this wind—it's here, but it's become background, something hardly worth noticing, much less commenting on.

"Deep thoughts?" Kalluk asked.

Tessa smiled up at him. "Not so deep. Just kind of recalling a trip I took to New York City."

"I've never been there. From what I've heard about it, I probably never will be."

"It's different from anywhere else in the world, I suppose. It's international—has a bit of everything, from high art to business to money to—"

"To drive-by shootings, street gangs, all sorts of dope,

homeless people sleeping in parks, crazies wandering around talking to themselves, carjackings," Kalluk finished her sentence.

"Any major city has those problems. It's not just New York. And I don't think the problems are quite as dire as you seem to think they are. There are lots of benefits to cities, Kalluk—the vitality, the diversity, all that."

"Yeah. I suppose that's true," he admitted begrudgingly. He nodded at the floor next to Tessa. "OK if I sit down for a while?"

"Sure."

Kalluk eased down next to her and sat Indian style. "But I think cities and all that's wrong with them have a big part in what I believe and what I do," he said.

"How so?"

"My people—my ancestors—lived for countless generations in peace with each other and with nature. We're not acquisitive people. Or, at least we never were until what's referred to as civilization in the lower 48 got here. Then, all of a sudden, many of us wanted—thought we needed—big-screen TVs, snowmobiles, credit cards, fancy houses." He peered into Tessa's eyes. "There's something enduring and powerful about the People," he went on. "I want to be part of saving them from whatever it is that civilization brings with it—greed or the need to imitate other groups and cultures because of the toys they have."

"I'm with you there," Tessa said. "That's why I'm an anthropologist. I think, though, that your scope is kind of narrow. What you said applies not solely to native Alaskans but all indigenous people—all those who're in culture shock because the new ways are rolling over them." She gazed into the fire for a moment and then posed a question. "What can you accomplish for the People?" she asked.

His eyes caught the reflection of the flames in their liquid chestnut darkness, and Tessa again felt as if she were being drawn into a whirlpool, whether she wanted to be or not.

"I can learn from them and about them. And I can take what I learn and give it back to others of my people and to anyone else who's interested in the purity of a lifestyle. That's exactly what I tell the young people when I speak at schools and colleges—that this pure and unhampered-by-possessions culture is on the cusp of fading away—and it's terribly important that we not let that happen."

"But Kalluk . . . is that really possible?"

He waved his hand almost angrily. "You don't get it—I'm not advocating all Inuits hunt seals with spears and eat whale blubber and live in huts they dig in the snow or build from slabs of ice." Kalluk took a breath. "Sorry, I didn't mean to snap at you. What we're talking about is important to me. And . . . and you're someone who understands. I *know* you are, and that's why I'm trying to make clear to you why I do what I do."

He took another breath, deeper this time. "You're a rare woman, Tessa. The way Fuzz took to you, the fact that you're here on this trek, the way you study and understand cultures and their importance—it makes you unique." He stood gracefully, without effort, at the same time breaking eye contact for the first time in minutes with Tessa. "We'll talk more," he said. Then he turned and walked over to the woodpile.

There's a lot to this man, Tessa thought as she watched him walk away. *What was the word he used? Unique? Yeah. He himself is unique—focused, deeply caring, on a mission that won't bring him any material gains. If only he were a bit less . . .*

R. E.'s "Hey, people—listen up!" drew everyone's attention to him. He stood from the log and put his back to the fire. "Today's been less than . . . um . . . delightful, right? Well, I have something here that'll adjust all of our attitudes, thanks to a certain lady." Playing the moment for all the drama he could squeeze out of it, R. E. slowly unbuttoned his heavy coat, reached into an inside pocket, and produced his Christmas gift Hershey bars. "I figured it out. Each of us will get two sections and part of another section."

"Are those . . . the ones with almonds?" Jessie asked, her voice reverent, as if she were asking for a personal loan—with no collateral—from the president of the World Bank.

R. E. nodded. "You betcha."

Even the brothers moved in from their spot beyond the fire. Neither chocolate nor coffee were indigenous to the state of Alaska, but they were the two substances Alaskans seemed to cherish the most. R. E. performed the surgery on the bars with Kalluk's nine-inch sheath knife. The chocolate was flint-hard from the cold, but it soon exuded its mystical, addictive sweetness on the tongues of the group. Randall spoke for all of them when he grunted, "Good."

Tessa nibbled tiny, crumblike pieces from her sections, making the chocolate last as long as possible. R. E., she noticed, was doing the same thing. Kalluk snapped his sections into smaller pieces with his fingers and ate them one at a time, as did Jessie. Albin and Randall's chocolate appeared as roundish lumps on the sides of their faces, reminding Tessa of an old farmer friend of her father's who always had a cud of chewing tobacco in place.

Kalluk, Tessa, and R. E. sat on folded blankets facing the fire, drinking from yet another pot of coffee, this one prepared by Tessa.

"This stuff would melt a railroad spike," R. E. commented.

"Only way to drink coffee is strong," Kalluk said. "I had an overpriced cup at one of those fancy coffeehouses with the cutesy names—'Grounds for Discussion' or something. It was awful. Dishwater."

"I can't quite see you in a yuppie gathering place," Tessa said. "Kinda like a grizzly bear at a tea party."

"You'd be surprised how civilized I can act." Kalluk grinned. "'Specially when I'm with a pair of grant officers from a foundation interested in Inuit studies."

"*Acting* is the operative word, I think," R. E. said. His voice carried no malice; in fact, Tessa thought she heard a tinge of jealousy to it.

"Whatever. I didn't get the grant, though, and I had to drink that horrid coffee."

Jessie was off to the side, scraping at the cave floor with a fist-sized, sharp-edged piece of rock. She was concentrating intently, the tip of her tongue just visible at the corner of her mouth. The stone-against-stone scratching caught Tessa's attention. "Whatcha doing, Jessie?" she asked.

Jessie gouged another line and sat back from her work. "Making a checkerboard. Looks like we're going to be here for a while. We need something to do."

Kalluk smiled. "You're not going to beat him, Jessie," he said.

Tessa and R. E. looked at Kalluk questioningly. "See," he said, "Jessie and Randall have been playing checkers for years, ever since she first hired the brothers for one of her trips. She's never beat him." After a pause, he added, "Probably never will. The guy is a machine when it comes to checkers. He never loses."

"He's lucky, is all," Jessie said.

"Right, Jess." Kalluk laughed. "He's been lucky for what— three or four hundred games in a row?"

"Doesn't matter. I've got his game figured out."

"I don't like to brag," Tessa said, "but my dad was a checkers champion, and he taught me everything he knew. I'm essentially unbeatable."

There was a single short bark of laughter from the semi-darkness where the brothers sat. Randall stood, grinning, his teeth white in the weak light. "We play," he said.

The pieces Jessie had collected were coin-sized, relatively flat bits of stone; half of them were gray, and the other pieces were almost black. She ran her hand across the scribed board and swept away the dust and crumbs of rock. "Randall?" she said.

Randall hunkered down across from her and arranged the gray pieces in front of him. Jessie did the same with the darker ones.

"I got the winner," Tessa called.

"Standard rules—best two out of three games," Jessie said.

Randall grunted affirmatively.

Randall beat Jessie two games to none; in the same fashion he dusted off Tessa, R. E., and Kalluk. Albin didn't play. Tessa came the closest to beating Randall, but he lured her into a pair of sucker moves, kinged three of his men, and swept over the scattered remnants of her forces like Sherman over Atlanta.

"I was just getting warmed up," Tessa said. "Next time . . ."

Randall grinned.

The floor of the cave had little to offer in terms of softness that night, but the tent floors kept the frigid surface from permeating flesh and bone. Although she was weary from the day, Tessa found sleep elusive. Her mind flitted from scene to scene, event to event. *R. E. shared his chocolate with the group. He didn't have to do it—but he did. It's a small thing, but a defining thing too.* She stirred uneasily, shifting the position of her body within the blanket she'd wound around herself.

Tessa moved again, looking for a bit of comfort she was unlikely to find. *I don't understand Kalluk. Maybe he's simply honest and says and does what his heart tells him to do. People who are as intense as he is tend to be that way—to express themselves regardless of the situation or circumstances.* She sighed aloud, and Fuzz, sleeping a foot or so from her, lifted his head at the sound. He watched her for several moments and then lowered his head back onto his forepaws.

What is it I feel about Kalluk? Fascination? Sure, he's an adventurer, a kind of figure from action-adventure fiction, a little bigger than life. There's more than that, though.

13

By the afternoon of the next day the woodpile was almost gone. The storm, however, seemed to continue to build. The wind was a ceaseless, manic shriek. Visibility was limited to a couple of feet, and less than that during yet more powerful gusts. Tessa peered through the brush and limbs that had been arranged at the cave's mouth, straining to see even vague forms or shapes with no success.

When she returned to the fire, Albin and Randall were bundling up for a trip outside for wood. Jessie, standing close to the brothers, leaned toward them and spoke quietly. After a moment, Albin nodded and reached under his coat. When Jessie turned from the brothers and toward Tessa, she was easing Albin's huge chromed pistol into the side pocket of her heavy coat. "There's no such thing as a sure thing out here," she said grimly to Tessa, "even with these guys. If something happened to both of them, the rest of us would be without protection, with no way to take game. My rifle is with the first trailer we lost."

Kalluk had wrapped a double loop of thin, plastic-coated

cable around his waist, and a large spool of the cable with a free end protruding rested at his feet. Randall tugged the free end up, wrapped it twice around his waist, and secured it with a knot that looked complicated to Tess, but took the man only a second to tie.

"What about Albin?" Tessa asked. "Won't he need a line?"

Kalluk's voice was tight when he answered. "Can't do it. We'd have to cut the cable to secure both of them, and that'd cut the distance they could travel in half. We're counting on there being wood along the banks of the stream. Albin will stay tight to Randall, maybe hang on to his coat if he needs to."

The brothers had moved to the mouth of the cave, Randall first. He crouched, eased forward, and ducked out into the storm. Albin followed on his brother's heels. In a matter of a few seconds they were swallowed by the weather; the only indication that they'd ever been there was the jerky unspooling of the cable. The four left behind stared at the spool as if it were a living thing trying to convey an important message to them through its gyrations.

The brothers seemed to be gone for an eon. It was, in actuality, fourteen minutes before the spool became silent and motionless.

"They're coming back," Jessie said. Her voice was breathy.

"Picking up wood as they come," Kalluk added. "That's the sensible way—a lot less distance to carry the load."

The return trip didn't take much longer than the initial one. Randall dumped a large armload of snow and ice-encrusted wood into the cave, and Albin did the same. The brothers came farther into the cave and headed for the fire. "Can you go out again?" Kalluk asked. "What you brought isn't going to last too long."

Albin looked at his brother for a moment before he spoke. "No. Tomorrow. We have wood for today and tonight."

"That bad out there?" Kalluk asked.

"Yes. Is that bad. We never seen storm like this."

Kalluk nodded. "Thanks, guys."

The new wood needed to be banged on the walls or floor of the cave to break away the clinging ice. Tessa saw that R. E. was cringing as he swung a limb at the wall. He must have felt her gaze; he half turned and winked at her.

It took a while for the frozen wood to catch fire, and before it did, it issued great clouds of steam as the existing flames licked at the water freed within the new fuel. The fire faltered as if a thick blanket had been thrown over it, but as the steam began to dissipate, the flames hungrily attacked the new fuel. R. E. and Tessa had stepped away from the cloud of steam and now moved back closer to the warmth of the fire. "Must have been rough out there if the brothers decided not to make a second trip," R. E. said.

"I remember a blizzard back home when I was a kid," Tessa said. "It lasted over four days. Cattle froze to death in their pastures. A woman—we didn't know her—was found afterward in a drift, not more than a few yards from her back door. I had nightmares about being lost in a storm for months after that."

R. E.'s gloved hand touched Tessa's arm comfortingly. "We're not in that kind of trouble, Tess. We have the best guides in the state with us. We'll get outta this just fine."

"Yeah," Tessa said, then added, "I know we will—I be-

193

lieve we will. Sometimes listening to that mess out there is depressing, though. When the brothers were getting wood I was scared for them and for all of us."

"'Course you were. Everyone was." R. E.'s face became grim. "I've talked to Jessie and Kalluk about the wood-gathering thing. Depending on how long the storm lasts, each of the men is going to be out there, hauling in wood—me included."

"Oh, R. E. Are you sure that's a good idea?"

"There's the safety line. That cable can't be broken by anything short of . . . I don't know. It's just a matter of being outside for maybe fifteen or twenty minutes. Even if a guy dropped unconscious out there, the rest of us could get to him or even haul him back to the cave with the cable." He stopped for a moment and took a breath. "I needed to tell you that, Tessa, so that it wouldn't be a huge surprise when it happened. OK?"

Tessa nodded her head slowly, her eyes avoiding R. E.'s. The words were difficult to set free, and she wasn't certain she believed them when she said, "It's a storm, not the end of the world. Storms come and go. You'll be fine—we'll be fine."

They drifted closer to the fire and sat on their blankets. Kalluk joined them after putting the coffeepot on the coals. Jessie was napping in the tent. The brothers huddled together in the semi-darkness beyond the fire. If they were speaking, they were doing it quietly, since no one else could hear them.

"Checkers, anyone?" R. E. asked.

"Nah, no thanks. I'm kind of checkered out," Kalluk said.

"Me too," Tessa added. She nudged the coffeepot with a

stick so that more heat got to its bottom. "I have an idea," she said. "Kalluk, isn't it true that the natives passed the long winters by telling stories? We can do that, can't we?"

"Well, yeah," Kalluk said. "But those were traditional, passed-down stories. The People had them pretty much memorized."

"OK," R. E. said. "But why can't we tell stories about ourselves? About things that happened to us when we were kids?"

Tessa's enthusiasm was only a tiny bit forced, but the stories, she thought, would be better than sitting there in silence, gawking into the fire. "That'll be fun. Kalluk—how about you starting?"

"I'd rather—"

"Come on!" R. E. and Tessa said in unison.

"OK. OK." He gathered his thoughts. "My great-grand-father was my hero when I was a kid. In a sense, he still is. The ol' man was tougher than a bull moose, and he followed traditional ways." He glanced at Tessa. "I lived with my grandparents until I was seventeen and went off to college on a 'Native Alaskan Promising Student' free-ride deal the state offered at the time. All through my childhood my great-grandfather would stop for a few days when he was in the area. My grandparents lived out in the boondocks, and my grandmother homeschooled me, so I had next to no association with other kids my age, Inuit or American. I spent most of my free time pretending I was Ve'an—that's both a name and a word in the dialect meaning "old one" or "wise one" or "grandfather"—hunting, tracking, building shelters, all that.

"Anyway, one time Ve'an spent almost a week with us. It

195

was the summer I was twelve. I was in heaven, following him around during the day, talking and learning from him, listening to his stories at night. We took a deer one day. Ve'an dropped it at a hundred yards or better with his 30.06 like it was nothing. We gutted the deer there and carried the meat and hide back home, about five miles or so. Remember, it was summer: the bugs were awful, clouds of them were around us, biting, buzzing, driving me crazy. I watched my grandfather as he walked. His face was totally impassive, even with the insects wading in the sweat. His stride never varied. I remember his eyes moved all the time, sweeping around and ahead of us, but other than that he might have been a shaggy robot lugging most of a deer on his back. I guess he felt me watching him so closely.

"Later that day we went to the general store in my grandfather's pickup. Ve'an let me drive after we were away from the house. When we got to the store, there were a half dozen or more Inuits standing and sitting in the shade of the building. They had a bottle of whiskey. They were loud and stupid and profane. Ve'an looked over at them as we went into the store, and the whole bunch of them got quiet in a big hurry. Same thing when we came out. There wasn't a sound from them. On the way home, Ve'an said, 'Those are not our People.' I was kind of confused—those guys were obviously Inuit, as my grandparents and Ve'an were. I started to ask a question, but my great-grandfather went on.

"'You watched me walk and you were proud of me, Kalluk. I know this to be true. And you wondered at how such an old man could shoot like that and carry meat through the bugs, through the heat.' I admitted I'd thought along those lines.

"'It was not only me you were proud of and not only me you loved,' Ve'an told me. 'It was our People you were seeing there, not a tired old man—our People who provide for themselves and their families, follow the seasons, live in friendship with nature, teach the young people the beauty of our way of life.

"'Those boys know none of that, Kalluk. Instead, they are foolish puppets, controlled by people not of their blood. Were the boys bad or evil? That's not for me to judge. But they were wrong. That's what matters here: they were wrong in what they were doing and how they are living.'

"Ve'an put his hand on my shoulder then. 'The People need the bright ones like you, Kalluk, the smart ones who can talk to others, make them understand who we are and how we live. If you and others like you don't do that, everything we know and believe and cherish will crumble away before your eyes. You must carry the message, Kalluk.'"

Kalluk was quiet for a long moment and then coughed rather self-consciously into his hand. "So, I've always considered that day a kind of pivotal point in my life. I never realize how clear all of it is in my mind until I start to tell it—then, I'm there all over again."

"Whew," Tessa breathed.

"Here's a nice lower 48 cliché I hesitate to use, Kalluk, but it fits perfectly here—thanks for sharing. It's a great story," R. E. said.

"Thanks. Who's next?" Kalluk asked.

"You're too hard an act to follow," Tessa said, standing. "I'll go next, but not now. OK?"

"Yeah," R. E. said. He rose from his blanket and stretched. "One thing we have is time."

197

"Wait a minute, here. That's unfair. The deal was that we'd all tell our stories. Like R. E. said, time is something we have plenty of. Come on—one of you has to go next."

R. E. and Tessa exchanged looks. After a moment they both sat down. Tessa took a breath and then began. "My story is about a focal point in my life too. The story is important because I think the experience I'm going to tell you about is one that kind of directed the rest of my life. This happened the summer I was thirteen." She picked up the coffeepot and topped off R. E.'s cup and Kalluk's and her own but continued speaking as she did so. "My mom and dad and I took a vacation that year. We'd always had short vacations, renting a cottage on a lake for a week, something like that. This year, though, we were driving to Wyoming. My dad had just bought a new Ford station wagon—we called it 'the land yacht,' it was that huge—to visit my mom's cousin and her family who lived in Pinedale, Wyoming, which is in the central part of the state. Right near there is the Wind River Indian Reservation, which is immense—over two million acres inhabited by Shoshone and Arapaho Indians. So, off we went in our shiny new wagon, with no actual time structure. My dad had saved up vacation time—and money—and we were going to explore for a month.

"It was a great trip. We stayed in motels, which was a big deal for me, and ate mostly junk food on the road, and saw all kinds of stuff. As we got closer to the reservation, though, the texture of everything seemed to change. There were ratty little stores selling what they called 'Indian crafts'—moccasins, dolls, carved figures, blankets, jewelry, trinkets, things like that. We stopped in a couple of the places, and my dad showed me the 'Made in Japan' labels on a bracelet and a

198

bunch of other items. The stores were run by Indians, and most of them rarely smiled. I thought they seemed embarrassed by what they were selling, and my mom agreed."

Tessa took a long gulp of coffee and used the time to order her thoughts. "The reservation was rough," she said. "It was painful to see. The shacks people lived in, the little children so listless and blank-eyed, men sitting around in that heat doing nothing. It went right to my dad's heart. I remember him saying, 'There's no one to speak for them, no one to help them, no one to understand them.' We went off the main roads and deeper into the reservation lands. Finally, we came to a little store with a single gas pump out in front of it. We all went in for soft drinks. There was an old Shoshone lady behind the counter. She looked ancient, except for her eyes. They were so deep a chestnut they were almost black, and they were as bright as those of a healthy child.

"My dad started talking with her—he's the type who can talk with anyone, because he's so interested in people—and we ended up sitting in front of the store under a canvas awning, drinking cold sodas. She told us about the reservation—she called it the res—and the poverty there, and the sickness and the child mortality rate and the hopelessness of the young men. We asked some questions, but mostly we listened. Finally, the lady said what it was that made me sure of what I wanted to do with the rest of my life. She said, 'The problem is, the outside world doesn't understand us or our ways. We've had hippies and writers and government people come through, and they talk and talk and don't listen, and then they're gone. What we need is someone who knows us to listen to us, to talk for us, to show who we are to the rest of the world.'

"That did it for me. I decided right then and there that I was going to be the person the old woman described, that I was going to learn about people and speak for those people, regardless of who or where they were." Tessa stood and stretched. "So there you have it. The turning point of my life, just like Kalluk's turning point was that day with his Ve'an."

"Thanks, Tessa," Kalluk said quietly.

"Great story, Tess," R. E. said. "Uh, how about I tell my tale tomorrow? It's short and isn't nearly as dramatic as either of yours. Maybe if I give it some thought tonight, I can embellish it a little, make it more—"

"Uh-uh, R. E.," Kalluk said. "We bared our souls. Now it's your turn."

"He's right, R. E.," Tessa said.

R. E. sighed. "Sure. Fair is fair. Like I said, this'll be short, but it's one of my strongest memories from my childhood." He cleared his throat and then began. "My folks were fairly wealthy. Upper middle class, I guess—we didn't have servants, but we had a new Buick or Olds every two years and a nice home and a pool, and we took great vacations. My dad was a lawyer—a tremendously hard worker, a bright and compassionate man, a great provider for his family, and a fine attorney. He was also rarely home. I was an only child, and I was close to my dad, or as close as I could be, considering the hours and the travel his work demanded. He had his first heart attack when I was seventeen, and the one that killed him when I was twenty-nine. Shortly after the first one, when he was home recuperating, we talked a lot. One evening he said to me, 'Don't let your life trap you, son. Consider what's important and what isn't.

200

Money isn't, and owning things isn't. Being at peace with yourself is.'"

R. E. cleared his throat again. "I remembered those words, but I still let my life trap me. I guess maybe I didn't realize that had happened until after my father passed on. But not too long ago I realized that I was trapped there in New York City."

"You're not trapped now, R. E.," Tessa said.

"No. I'm not." He looked into the fire. "And I lived on in Alaska happily ever after, or assume I will, anyway. End of story. Everyone ready to hit the tents?" R. E.'s words were quick and self-conscious. The three of them got to their feet silently, gathered up their blankets, and said their good nights without further conversation.

Jessie was sleeping soundly when Tessa entered their tent. Jessie had obviously stretched her catnap into her sleep for the night. It was just as well. Tessa didn't much care to talk just then. The stories she'd heard and the one she'd told were in her mind.

I haven't been so intimate with anyone—man or woman—in a long time, Tessa thought. *Maybe not since my college days when I'd talk with my roommate and friends and drink gallons of coffee from evening till morning and then drag myself off to classes in a daze.*

I feel like I know these men better now. They're both good guys, each in his own way.

14

On the third day of the storm Kalluk went out for wood. He was out longer than Albin and Randall had been, and when he started back only a few feet of cable remained on the spool. He dumped a satisfyingly large load of wood in the cave, but his face was a milky white, his eyes red, and his lips gray. Jessie put a mug of coffee between his gloved hands, and Kalluk accepted it clumsily, his fingers wooden and uncoordinated. The hot liquid slopped over the edge of the cup as he lifted it to his mouth. It was steaming hot, but Kalluk took a large swallow, as if it were cold soda on a very hot day. Even so, it was several moments before he could speak. "I never saw anything like this," he mumbled through numbed lips. "I thought I'd seen the worst. I hadn't."

The brothers nodded in agreement as they hauled wood to the pile.

"I had to go farther out than I thought I would," Kalluk said. "And the snow's deeper—several feet along the streambed, taller than I am where it's drifted. I spent most of my time digging." He gulped more coffee, moving a bit more freely now. "R. E.," he said, "when you go out, turn left at the mouth. I went right, and that area's been pretty much picked over."

"Yeah. OK. I'll do that," R. E. said.

"And don't go getting lost," Tessa said, half serious, half laughing.

Both Kalluk and R. E. turned to look at her. Tessa could feel their gazes on her face. Then she felt the heat of a blush in her cheeks. *Why are they both looking at me like that?*

A few minutes later, Jessie touched her shoulder. "C'mon with me. I need to talk to you about something," she said. They walked past the fire, into the area beyond the glow of it, where the light was dark and grainy.

Jessie sighed and turned to face Tessa. "I watch things on these trips, Tess—I have to," she said. "I especially watch eyes. That ol' thing about eyes being the window to the soul is absolutely gospel true. I've had romances and rivalries spring up on my treks, and I've seen how they can tear up the concept of a team and turn folks into separate little guarded camps. That's no good when things are going well, and in a situation like ours, it's downright dangerous to all of us."

A gust outside shifted direction, rattling the branches in the cave mouth and reaching far enough inside to ruffle the fire, putting a shower of sparks in the air.

Jessie took a half step closer to Tessa. "What are your feelings toward R. E.?" she asked. Before Tessa could answer, Jessie added, "I'm not prying here, Tess. It's my responsibility to get all of us back to Fairview in one piece. I have to know what's going on between my people, undercurrents and all."

"He's an interesting man—a good man," Tessa answered honestly. "He's funny and smart, one of the kindest people I've ever met. I like being with him."

"Are you in love with him?"

"I care about him. Maybe I could love him someday."

"What about Kalluk?"

"I don't know. He's fascinating, of course—and charismatic. I suppose I'm a little attracted to him."

"Mmmm. You and a thousand other women," Jessie said quietly. "And you must know that Kalluk hasn't really chased them away with a stick."

"Yeah. Meeloa said something like that to me."

"I can't say that Kalluk's a womanizer. I don't think he actually is. I do think he's searching for a partner, and that as gruff and independent as he seems, he's kind of lonely. Men who're as driven as he is are like that."

Tessa didn't respond. Jessie sighed and then continued. "Here's the thing, though: you've got two men who care for you—probably are in love with you. R. E. definitely is, and I think Kalluk is too. For now, though, you've got to put all that aside, 'cause we've still got to get out of here and back to the sleds alive, or none of that will make any difference at all. After we're safe, none of this will be any of my business, and I'll forget we had this conversation. But until that time, all I'm asking is that you be careful around them, don't show one of them more attention than the other, and everything will be ... ummm ... harmonious. OK?"

Tessa nodded. "I'm not sure you're right about their feelings toward me, but yeah, I'll be careful."

After Kalluk had unhitched himself and respooled the cable, Tessa and Jessie joined him and R. E. at the fire. Albin and Randall, as usual, hung back several feet from the others.

Jessie turned to address them all. "We're not doing real good on food," she said. "We're going to have to share MREs tonight, one to each two people. We still have coffee and some canned fruit, but not much else. The boys can't hunt in the storm, so we'll have to stretch what we have. There's a two-pound block of cheese for two meals tomorrow, and MREs for tomorrow night. Everyone needs to keep on drinking water to avoid dehydration." She looked around the cave, catching each traveler's eye for a moment. "Questions? Anybody have anything to say? Any ideas to make things better here at the Alaska Hilton?"

R. E. finally broke the silence that was beginning to stretch uncomfortably. "How long can this mess last, Jessie? Will we be able to find the sleds after we get out of here? With all the snow we've had, it seems like they'll be deeply covered."

"We'll find the sleds," Jessie said. "The basic landmarks—that huge tree with the crooked trunk, the boulder, the rise to the northeast—won't change no matter how deep the snow is. Kalluk and I both triangulated the position of the sleds." She hesitated for a few seconds. "As to how long the storm can last, I have no idea. I listened to the wind this morning. It's still screaming like a banshee out there, and the snow is as thick as ever. Kalluk, what do you think?"

"I don't know." He shook his head. "I thought the winds would be slowing down by now, but that's not happening."

Jessie looked over at the brothers. "Albin? Randall?"

Albin, responding for both of them, made a palms-up, "beats me" gesture.

"OK, then," Jessie said, ending the impromptu meeting. "Let's stay as warm as we can. Anyone other than Randall want to play some checkers?"

━◆━

That night, tired and cold, and now with an additional woe, hunger, Tessa huddled under her blanket on the tent floor next to Jessie, who, as usual, had gone to sleep as soon as she closed her eyes. Over the pleasant crackle of the fire and the occasional shifting of a chunk of wood as it was consumed, Tessa listened to the ravings of the storm.

So, we're short on food, but we have a decent fire, and there seems to be enough wood out there to keep it going. A growl from her stomach brought a small smile to her face. *Like I said, we're short on food. As soon as they can see what they're doing out there, Albin and Randall will go hunting. Funny how my perspective has changed on that. I'd eat a rabbit or duck or goose or whatever the brothers shot right now, and not give the animal another thought, not any more than I mourned for the cow when I ate a burger back in the lower 48.*

Tessa's hunger conjured up the image of a large piece of meat skewered over open flames, fat dripping and hissing in the fire, sending up smoke that tickled her nose with the scent of cooking meat. *Stop!* she mentally chided herself. *Think of something else.*

That wasn't terribly hard to do when she put her mind to it. *Tomorrow, R. E. goes out for wood. The brothers and Kalluk have done it, and now he believes it's his turn, and I guess it is. Anyway, the cable will keep him safe, but I'm still nervous about it.*

207

Maybe the storm will blow out tonight, and we can start back to the sleds. Tessa snorted. *Maybe the bluebird of happiness will carry me gently back to Fairview too, and have a hot bath and a huge meal waiting for me when we get there.*

I wonder . . . was Jessie right about R. E.'s and Kalluk's feelings toward me? R. E. has always been attentive to me, and he's the sweetest guy in the world, but I never felt he was falling in love with me. Now, when I think of some of the things he's said on the trip, I'm not so sure. And, what about Kalluk? He's the strong, silent type but Jessie knows him well, and she thinks he sees me as a potential life partner. As Tessa drifted into sleep, an interesting proposition formed at the edge of her consciousness: *If I had to make a choice, which one would I choose—R. E. or Kalluk?*

Someone added wood to the fire, being none too quiet in the process. The sibilant hiss of escaping steam followed as the wood released moisture into the flames. Tessa followed the sound, not quite asleep but far from fully conscious. It led her to a good place, a warm and secure one, and images of her time in Alaska floated past her—the herd of elk she'd seen with R. E., the magnificent northern lights and their beautiful palette of colors, the rugged and impervious peak of Mt. McKinley touching the sky. She saw herself with Meeloa, laughing with the elders after her unconscious attempt at throat singing, saw herself in the mercantile at a table with R. E., giggling about something silly. The memory of the first time she'd seen and spoken to Kalluk flashed in her mind, his quiet strength, his presence that seemed dramatic even when he was talking casually.

Tessa's life back home—the images from that time—jarred her almost to wakefulness. She saw herself grading

208

papers, lecturing to young people whose eyes showed their acute boredom as they struggled to stay awake. She found herself at a faculty party, listening to a pontificating department head who'd hit the white wine a tad too hard.

Tessa felt the campus sidewalk under her shoes as she walked home after classes on a spectacular autumn afternoon when the colors of the changing trees were so vivid, so alarmingly beautiful, that the panorama brought a lump to her throat, as did the realization that she had no one with whom to share all that natural glory.

The department head at the party snuck back into her mind. He was leaning forward, almost but not quite insinuating himself into her personal space. She moved uncomfortably under her blanket.

Her lips formed a silent oath: "No. Never again. That won't be my life."

The next morning, when Tessa awoke, something was different, but she couldn't quite place what it was. She pulled the blanket more tightly around herself, buying a few more moments of dozing. The sounds around her were the ones she'd become accustomed to: Jessie and Kalluk's quiet voices, Fuzz noisily lapping water out of a used MRE tray, the whispering of the fire as it eased to daytime embers. The wind . . .

She sat bolt upright and looked toward the mouth of the cave, where the brothers stood, their backs to her and their heads together. The wind had a totally different tone to it, a far less frantic, more subdued, infinitely less threatening tone.

"'Bout time you got up, Sleeping Beauty," Jessie said as she poured some coffee. Her face had the smile of a child on

Christmas morning. Tessa didn't need to ask the question: Jessie gave the answer before she could speak. "It's dying, Tess. The storm is almost over."

R. E., next to Jessie, held out his hand. Tessa took it, and he pulled her to her feet. He beamed at her without speaking, his eyes conveying his joy and his relief. Kalluk looked over from across the fire, smiling. "It's still snowing like mad, but there's no teeth left to this storm." He proudly held up a skinned rabbit. "Look what Fuzz brought us this morning. I'm just getting it ready for the fire."

"Good ol' Fuzz!" Tessa exclaimed. "But he's been hungry too. How come he didn't chow down on that rabbit?"

"Look at him." Kalluk laughed. "See how his stomach is hanging? The blood all over his chest and muzzle? He helped himself to at least one other rabbit before he brought this one to us."

The mood, the relief from tension, was infectious—as welcome as the aroma of the cooking meat was to the hungry group. Albin and Randall refused their shares. Randall tapped the lump below his left armpit. "We hunt soon," he promised.

The snowshoe hare was a good-sized animal—twenty-four inches long and weighing about five pounds. The meat, savory and white, like that of a chicken, was an inordinately welcome change from MREs. Tessa tore into her piece, just as R. E., Jessie, and Kalluk did theirs. They grinned at one another as they gnawed, ignoring their greasy chins and lack of utensil use.

R. E., sated, tossed the bone he'd been chewing clean into the fire. "Time to saddle up," he said. "Gotta go out and play in the snow."

"But, the storm's almost over, isn't it?" Tessa protested.

"Almost doesn't mean completely, Tess," Jessie said. "Look at how skimpy our woodpile is, and we're going to have to spend at least tonight here."

Tessa walked beside R. E. toward the front of the cave. "I wish you didn't have to go out there," she said quietly.

"No big deal. No matter what happens, you people could haul me back in, right?"

They crouched behind the brush at the cave mouth. The snow was no longer wind-driven, but it was falling so heavily that it looked like an impenetrable white screen. They stared out for a moment, silent. Tessa began to reach out to touch R. E.'s hand but never completed the motion. *Don't show one of them more attention than the other.*

Kalluk wrapped the cable twice around R. E.'s waist, set the clasp, and pulled against it, making certain it was secure. "Ready?" he asked. "You'll go left, right?"

"Right." R. E. smiled.

"No, left."

"Right."

"No . . ."

"You boys are a laugh riot," Jessie commented sarcastically, breaking the routine. "Cut the nonsense. Remember, R. E.—it's still about thirty degrees below zero out there. Move slowly and don't try to carry more than you can handle comfortably."

R. E. nodded, crouched again, and pushed his way through the cave mouth into the snow. The spool moved erratically at first but leveled off to smooth, slow revolutions. Those left in the cave stared at it as if its movement revealed the secrets and mysteries of the universe. R. E. was making his way more slowly—and probably more cautiously—than Kalluk or Albin and Randall had. After several minutes, Jessie went back to tend the fire, and the brothers wandered to their spot just barely within the light cast by the flames.

Kalluk cleared his throat, probably needlessly, Tessa observed. They were standing a foot or so apart, side by side. "We haven't talked since the other day," he said.

"No, we haven't."

Kalluk moved a couple inches closer to Tessa; she moved back the same distance.

"I know I seem to come on awfully strong, Tessa. That's the way I do things, and I won't apologize for it."

When Tessa began to respond, Kalluk held up a hand. "Please let me say what I've got to say, OK?" He cleared his throat again, and his eyes locked on hers. As always, the intensity and directness of his gaze was disorienting. She nodded.

"I know you think all of what I'm going to say is too fast and that I don't know you or anything about you. I don't think that's true—and I don't think it's important, either."

Kalluk began to reach for her, perhaps to hold her shoulders, but stopped in midmotion and lowered his hands to his sides. "The People I come from know nothing of dating or the other lower 48 rituals. They think they're silly. Marriages were either arranged by parents or grandparents, or a man and a woman would meet and be joined in marriage a few days later."

Tessa began to protest, and again Kalluk halted her.

"My point is that I feel . . . strongly . . . about you. I'd like to ask—"

"Kalluk! Where are you going with all this? I don't—"

"Please, Tessa, let me finish." He sighed. "What I do is important to me and to my people. I'm not going to change that—wouldn't change it if I could. That doesn't mean I don't have an open space next to me that I want to fill with a woman—a partner in all things. I've been looking for that partner for a long time. A couple of times I thought I'd found her. I was wrong. Those women—Inuits, expatriate lower 48ers, whatever—either knew nothing of the People, or worse, cared nothing about them. You do care, and you've made wonderful efforts to get to know and understand them."

"But I'm an anthropologist. It's my job to study people and cultures."

"Whatever," he said dismissively. "Your culture—your ways—are different from mine. Fine. I realize that. But tell me this—can you honestly say that you haven't felt attracted to me since we've met? If you haven't, I'll end this right now and never mention it again, if that's what you want."

"Kalluk—this is so sudden, so . . . I don't know . . ."

"Are you going to answer my question?"

"No . . . no."

"No, you won't answer my question, or no you don't feel anything for me?"

Tessa took a breath before speaking. "Stop grilling me, Kalluk. This isn't fair. I need to think about everything—where I'm going and what I'm going to do. I hope you didn't actually expect me to leap on your invitation or proposal or whatever it was."

"OK. Fair enough. But, two days after we get back to Fairview I'm going to come to you. We'll talk about all this again. Until then, nothing. OK?"

213

Tessa didn't get a chance to respond because Kalluk pressed his lips against hers, held her for a moment longer, and then turned and walked toward the fire. She stood there, stunned, staring at Kalluk's back. When he picked up a chunk of wood and pitched it into the flames, he avoided meeting her eyes. She was still a bit dazed when Albin and Randall appeared next to her, looking down at the now unmoving spool. Tessa hadn't noticed that it'd stopped its clattering revolutions on the uneven floor. "Coming back," Randall pointed out needlessly.

Albin picked up the spool and rewound the slack cable onto it, stopping every so often to avoid putting any tugging pressure on R. E. After what seemed like an unbearably long time to Tessa, Albin set the spool down, and he and Randall moved to the mouth of the cave, pulling aside the brush and limbs. R. E. dumped his load of wood and flapped his arms to get the circulation running properly in them. His face was red, and his breathing a little too fast and a little too loud. The amount he'd carried was large—at least equal to what Kalluk had hauled in. R. E. obviously realized that, and his smile was a proud one.

"Are you OK?" Tessa asked. "You sound beat."

R. E.'s hands hung at his sides, his mittenlike gloves now lumps of crusted snow and ice. Tessa freed the scarf from around his face and neck and began to unbutton his heavy coat. His lips, tight blue lines, contrasted with the red flush of his face. "I mighta pushed it a little," he admitted; his voice was not much more than a gasp.

Jessie held a mug of steaming coffee to his face, letting him sip. Her face mirrored her concern. "Take a deep breath, R. E.," she instructed. He swallowed a mouthful of coffee

214

and then did so. "Let it out slowly," she told him. She inclined her ear toward R. E.'s mouth, listening as the breath was expelled. "Good," she said when she straightened and stepped back. "Doesn't sound like you did any damage to your lungs. But look—for future reference, carrying too heavy a load is as bad for you as running in this kind of weather."

Albin and Randall slipped by the others wordlessly and crouched to leave the cave. Since their weapons were unholstered and in their hands, muzzles pointed toward the floor, there was no question about where they were going. "No MREs tonight," Kalluk commented. "Probably rabbit again. They're about the only creatures out."

"Whatever's not holed up, those boys will bring back," Jessie said.

R. E. was a bit unsteady on his feet, Tessa thought as they walked to the fire. He stood close to the flames, holding out his hands over them, working his fingers, forming and releasing fists. Steam began to rise from his boots, which were almost touching the coals. "Whew," he said.

"Come on and sit down," Tessa said. R. E. sat Indian-style at her side, staying close to the warmth. Jessie and Kalluk were slamming pieces of frozen wood against the cave wall.

"I was worried about you," Tessa said when there was a break in the racket.

R. E. turned to face her. "That's nice to hear."

Jessie and Kalluk laughed together about something, and Tessa and R. E. looked their way for a moment. When Tessa looked back, R. E.'s eyes were fixed on her.

"I know that he's fancier than I am, Tess," he said in a low voice.

"Fancier? I don't know what you mean."

"Sure you do. No one could miss it. He's the type of man everyone notices, everyone kind of admires. An icon, in a sense—doing great things, flying around in bush planes, hanging around with people who live as they did two or three or more centuries ago—all that."

"You're every bit as fancy as Kalluk is." She couldn't help it. She giggled at her use of the word *fancy*. After a moment, so did R. E.

"But still," he went on, "the guy looks like some kind of action hero from Hollywood. I've seen women of all ages walk into the store and it's suddenly like I'm not even there. All eyes go to him, even if he's just sitting at a table drinking coffee."

"Looks are only looks. They're not the person." She leaned forward. "And you aren't half-bad yourself." She grinned mischievously. "In fact, back at the university, the girls would refer to you as a hottie."

R. E.'s proud grin was that of a little boy who just batted the winning run in the ninth inning of a tied baseball game. He glanced over toward Kalluk and Jessie and spoke a little more hurriedly. "When we get back, we'll talk. OK?"

"Sure. We'll talk when we get home."

Branches shifted at the mouth of the cave, and a large snowshoe hare plopped ungracefully to the floor, followed by another. Jessie and Kalluk cheered as Albin emerged into the cave, followed closely by Randall. "Good stew," Randall said, his face as impassive as those on Mt. Rushmore.

There was a tingle of anticipation in the cave for the balance of the day. Freedom from the dank cell they'd spent so much time in loomed ahead of each of them like a promise. Even the brothers seemed the slightest bit nervous; they moved about more than they ordinarily did, poking at the fire, cleaning and recleaning their handguns.

R. E. and Jessie began a checkers series, but both quickly lost interest in the game. Tessa watched logs in the fire be consumed, which, she realized, was not unlike watching grass grow or paint dry.

Conversations were started but didn't last long. Jessie napped, R. E. gazed off into space, Kalluk scratched Fuzz's back, the brothers talked quietly to one another in their native language, and Tessa found herself jolting awake from a very shallow sleep when a log shifted in the fire.

The evening meal was a broth-and-meat combination, and it was very good. When they'd all finished eating, Jessie and Kalluk put their heads together for a few moments. Kalluk stood. "Let's get some shut-eye, folks—looks like we're going to be able to start back at first light."

Tessa was more tired than she could recall being even during the early days of the trek, yet sleep eluded her. Her wakefulness, though, wasn't the restless sort—instead, it was generated by a conglomeration of thoughts and emotions that needed the silence and the unobtrusive, mellow light cast by the night-banked fire.

One thing I'm certain of now: I won't go back to Minnesota and to the university. That life was then; this one is now. Alaska has me right by the heart.

Reality crept in, at least for a moment. *How'll I support myself? The university will pull the cabin as soon as I resign. And the Jeep and everything else.*

I can write articles for anthro journals, tutor kids, teach via correspondence—whatever. What do I need? A place to live, food, a beater of a vehicle that at least runs, that's about it.

A curious scraping sound got Tessa's attention. She pushed away her blanket and raised herself on an elbow. Fuzz was whining quietly, as if he was dreaming, and his legs flinched in a semblance of running. *Hunting? Running from something? What are wolf-dogs afraid of?* She smiled. *He sure took to me, though. That seemed to start when Kalluk left him the night the bear trashed my cabin—Fuzz started bringing me gifts.* She sighed. *Funny how perceptions can change.*

R. E. and Kalluk. I've never really sought a man. I thought it'd happen sometime, but I wasn't craving a relationship above all else in my life. Then I met R. E. There could be a whole lot there.

The stark contradiction of her next thought prodded Tessa. *What about Kalluk? Is that infatuation on my part? A nonsensical attraction? How could he know I'm the one in such a short time? His sincerity, delusional or not, shows so clearly in his eyes. What will I say to Kalluk when he shows up at my door—and he will—back in Fairview? Is this the one time in my life when I shouldn't be an analytical, practical woman?*

For that question, she had no real answer.

The trek back to the sleds began on a morning that could have appeared on a travel poster. The sky was a lush blue, deep, with the clarity of color of a perfectly cut blue topaz. The wind was blessedly still; a dropped handful of snow drifted to the ground languidly. The individual flakes found their own meandering ways downward, as if teasing the call of gravity. The air, after their days in the dank and smoke-tainted cave, was pristine and new and tasted of sunshine and life. Each of the travelers, including Albin and Randall, stood outside the cave for long, silent moments, letting the cleanliness wash over them, drawing the freshness into their bodies, renewing themselves.

Almost four feet of snow had fallen during the storm, but the crazed, never-still wind had rarely allowed it to accumulate to that height. Instead, it'd formed weird and precarious mounds and free-form sculptures that towered over them in places, like geologic features of some new and unexplored planet.

"It's warmed up a lot," Tessa observed.

Jessie chuckled. "It's the lack of wind." She checked her thermometer and grinned. "But you're right—the temp has skyrocketed all the way up to nineteen below zero."

"It's a heat wave," R. E. said. "Maybe we can find a place to swim and have a picnic."

Tessa was forming a response when Kalluk cut in. "Hey, people—glare is going to be a real problem today. Unless you use eye protection, your vision will be shot within a few hours."

Tessa and R. E. looked at one another—both pairs of their sunglasses had scudded off into the storm in the whisked-away trailer. Jessie was already wearing hers, and Kalluk was adjusting his own.

"Ours are gone," R. E. said. "Maybe we can squint or something."

Jessie walked over to the brothers. Within minutes they had their sheath knives out and were carefully carving slits into pieces of wood about four inches long. To the ends of the pieces of wood they attached rawhide thongs. Albin motioned Tessa to him. He stepped behind her, placed the carved wood over her eyes, and tied the thong at the back

219

of her head. Randall finished carving and did the same for
R. E.

"This is amazing," Tessa said. "It's like wearing real sunglasses."

"It's the same principle that lets us look at a solar eclipse
through a pinhole device without hurting our eyes," Kalluk
explained. "That tiny slit Albin and Randall cut into the
pieces of wood lets very little light in and cuts the glare
way down."

"Stylish too," R. E. commented. "We look like a pair of
space aliens."

Kalluk and Jessie set what seemed to be a reasonable but
rapid pace to Tessa and R. E., at least for the first hour or
so. Then, it became a grueling speed-walk sort of challenge.
The brothers ranged a hundred or so yards ahead, frequently
going out of sight of the others. Tessa and R. E. trudged
side by side, fifteen feet behind Kalluk and Jessie.

"We gotta tell them to slow down," R. E. panted.

"Don't breathe through your mouth. Let's give it a little
more time."

Jessie dropped back about forty-five minutes later, looked
at Tessa and R. E., and took several strides to catch up to
Kalluk. She said something to him, and he stopped immediately. Both he and Jessie returned to Tessa and R. E. Out
toward the horizon the brothers stood together, looking
back at the others.

"We'll take a break here for a bit," Kalluk said. "I'm sorry,
Tessa and R. E. You should have said something. You're
both as red as beets."

"It's my fault too," Jessie said. "I should have paid more
attention to you two. I heard you talking earlier and figured

you were OK with the pace. Kalluk and me, we're used to
. . . never mind. That changes nothing. Don't sit down yet.
Your muscles will set up if you do. Keep walking around in
big circles nice and slow until we get some coffee brewed.
Then you can rest."

Tessa and R. E. nodded, both too breathless to speak.
They walked off slowly, their boots dragging. Kalluk, who'd
been pulling the trailer, used the scraps of wood he'd loaded
to start a small fire.

It was close enough to lunchtime, they all decided. Jessie
added ground coffee to the pot and edged MREs into the
fire. R. E. met the brothers as they came in. Kalluk hunkered
down next to Tessa where she sat on the closed lid of the
almost empty trailer.

"You feel OK?" Kalluk asked. "We have maybe three hours
and some minutes left of the light for the day. If you and
R. E. are too worn out, we could move closer to the forest
and camp for the night."

"We're fine, Kalluk—really. And spend extra time out here
when we can be snowmobiling to Fairview? No sir."

"Had enough of wilderness treks, eh?" Kalluk asked.

"Not nearly," Tessa said. "This is a disappointment, but it's
not the end of the world. I'll be out here or places like here
dozens of times before I'm finished. I've learned a lot on this
trip. Even with the problems, it's been good for me."

"Oh? How?"

"I've made the decision that I'll never leave Alaska, for
one thing. And that I have what it takes to make a decent
number of treks like this. Sure, I'm a newbie. But I didn't ask
for or expect any special consideration, and I've kept up."

"Yeah. You have." Kalluk ran a gloved finger over the

snow in front of him, creating a circuitous little path like that of a miniature bobsled run. When he looked up, his eyes met Tessa's. "I never doubted you'd tough out the trip. And the fact that you've fallen in love with Alaska is no surprise, either."

Tessa broke eye contact and glanced away. R. E. was walking back toward her. Kalluk rose in that same graceful, effortless motion Tessa had noticed several times before.

"Albin and Randall promised us a good dinner," R. E. said. "Randall thinks some Canada geese will be moving after the storm."

The balance of the day was much like the first days of walking to Tessa. She felt the fatigue not only in her legs and feet but in the length of her spine. The terrain was decent for walking, but the group periodically encountered long, deep drifts that were too lengthy to go around. They battered their way through, Albin and Randall generally breaking a path, but plowing through knee deep was far from an easy amble. When Kalluk called a stop for the night, Tessa was grateful.

Better than a half hour after they'd made camp and had a fire going, the brothers came in. Albin carried a goose slung over his shoulders. Tessa had no familiarity with the big Canada geese other than hearing and seeing them fly over her Minnesota home in their familiar V formation. She'd never seen one close up and was amazed at the size of the one the brothers had shot. The goose weighed about sixteen pounds, and its body, from head to tail feathers, was at least four feet long. There was plenty of meat in the pot that evening, and thick chunks of it were skewered on sticks and baked directly over the flames. The flesh was rich, slightly but not unpleasantly gamey-tasting, and as filling as sirloin steaks would have been.

The camp went silent not long after the meal was finished. Tessa and Jessie crept into their tent while the fire was still high. R. E. and Kalluk arranged the balance of the wood at the periphery of the fire, and then they, too, turned in.

Tessa wrestled with conflicting images in her mind of R. E. and Kalluk, but those didn't last long before the exhaustion of the day dropped her into a deep and dreamless sleep.

The second day of the trip to the sleds dawned with the spectacular clarity and beauty that causes even the natives to stop what they're doing and marvel at the perfection of nature. The established pace was a good one—not overly slow for Kalluk and Jessie, and not overly fast for R. E. and Tessa. The makeshift sunglasses were again necessary. The brothers scouted ahead and were beyond the horizon for much of the day. The echoing report of a pistol shot at midday announced that lunch wouldn't be long in coming, and the group was ready for food and some moments of rest when Albin and Randall came trudging in, a fat hare slung over Albin's shoulder. It was the second day devoid of wind or even a breeze; the bluish white smoke from fat dripping onto the flames of the campfire ascended in an almost perfectly straight line, but the aroma of the broiling meat and the pungent scent of brewing coffee seemed to spread forever in all directions.

Tessa found herself fantasizing that afternoon as she strode along next to R. E. Pizza had always been a big favorite of

hers, almost to the point of becoming a benign addiction.
All of the student help and the owners of Paulie—Prince of
Pizza, a small shop just off campus—knew her by her first
name, and had her preferred topping memorized. There
was no pizza parlor in Fairview, nor was there one within a
hundred and fifty miles of Fairview. As a consequence, Tessa
hoarded the slightly cardboard-tasting frozen pizza pies
R. E. received at his store on an irregular basis. She craved
one now—not a slice, but the entire pizza—with a yearning
that was generating a wave of saliva in her mouth.

She saw the skimpy little shower stall in her cabin, and
in her mind it was the equal of the most lavish bathroom in
any copy of *Architecture Today*. In reality, the cabin facility
was a selfish, spitting showerhead much prone to swinging
from scalding hot water to icy cold with no warning, with
pipes that rattled and banged as if they were trying to escape
from their dark prisons behind moldy Sheetrock and lathe.
But even those feeble accommodations were far superior to
the hurried, goose-bumpy washcloth baths that left her with
chattering teeth and feeling not much cleaner.

She fixated on her bed, her fireplace, her refrigerator
with its bounty of delights such as cheese and bacon and
beef—and the cupboard where, behind a sack of flour, her
giant-sized bag of Peanut M&M's awaited her. A conversation with R. E. flitted through her mind:

"Nuts are supposed to be in cans or little cellophane bags,"
he said, "not in bread or muffins or under a thin, crisp,
candy shell, messing up the concept of the original and
real M&M's."

"What a geek," she'd commented.

"What?" R. E. asked, pulling Tessa back to the present.

"What what?"

"You were kind of off in the twilight zone for a few minutes, and then all of a sudden you were laughing."

"I was just thinking of something funny."

"C'mon, you got to tell me. I could use a laugh."

"It's silly. How about this: I'll tell you when we're sitting in front of my fireplace drinking hot cocoa in a few days, OK?"

"Sounds good to me. I'll look forward to it."

They came upon the snowmobiles in the early afternoon of the next day. The sleds and the rock face they were parked next to were under several feet of snow, but the landmarks Jessie and Kalluk had used for their triangulation remained readily visible. The snow was almost weightless, and even when packed and compressed by the winds of the storm, it was easy to clear. Jessie took a can of aerosol ether from the tool kit of one machine while Kalluk opened the engine cowls and removed the air filters, leaving the carburetors uncovered. Jessie hissed a long spray of ether into the carburetor of the first sled as Kalluk hauled on the starter cord. The engine coughed, fired, raced for a moment, and then settled down to an even idle. The second snowmobile was more recalcitrant, but after several strong yanks on the cord and hits of ether, the engine grumbled to life.

Twenty-six hours later, ears buzzing from the constant racket of the sled engines, faces raw from fighting the wind generated by their speed, Tessa, R. E., Jessie, Kalluk, Albin, and Randall pulled to the rear of R. E.'s mercantile emporium.

The trip was over.

15

The meat-locker chill in Tessa's cabin hadn't yet backed down in the face of the roaring fire she'd built in the fireplace before she was standing under her showerhead, luxuriating in the hot water pummeling her. She lathered and rinsed her hair three times before it gave a satisfying squeak as she rubbed a lock between her thumb and forefinger. She scrubbed her body with the thick suds of a fresh bar of Irish Spring and then used her loofah as if she were sanding away the grime of two weeks away from normal bathing facilities. When the hot water finally ran out, her skin was tingling pleasantly, and she was reveling in the exuberant joy of feeling genuinely clean after being not-so-clean for an extended period of time.

Warmth from the fire had risen upstairs as Tessa dressed in wonderfully fresh-smelling jeans, flannel shirt, and thick woolen socks. It was then that the demanding, voracious craving for pizza struck. She hustled downstairs, tossed more wood into the fireplace even though the fire was already well beyond the conservative size she usually built, and removed a pizza from the freezer of her refrigerator. She unwrapped it carefully, doing her best not to dislodge any of the big coins of pepperoni scattered over its surface. Even frozen, the pie exuded a scent that brought hungry grumbles from her stomach.

As the pizza baked, Tessa looked through her accumulated mail. In Minnesota, after a long absence she'd have come home to a bale of junk, catalogs, and mail-order scams. Here in Alaska, her new home, her mail consisted of a paycheck from the university, a letter from the head of the anthro department, and a note from a favorite aunt.

The pizza was flamboyantly delicious, and the Diet Coke she drank with it was cold and sweet and as good as the TV commercials claimed it to be. She pushed her chair back from the table, patted her stomach, and smiled. "This is good," she said aloud. "This is very good."

Sleep didn't come nearly as quickly and as easily as Tessa had anticipated. She wondered about that as she tossed about on her queen-sized bed. When she realized that the bed felt too soft to her after all her nights on a tent floor on the tundra, she smiled. *I'll get used to it* was her last thought for the night.

There was a pervasive edge of nervousness prodding Tessa the next day. She found herself stopped in midmotion with her soapy cereal bowl in her hands, staring blankly out the window over her sink.

Kalluk said he'd be here tonight. And I have a feeling Kalluk always does what he says he's going to do. He's going to want an answer. But the question is absurd: will I leave everything

I know and care about to chase around the biggest state in the union with a radical activist whom I've known for a month or so? Of course not. But, what are my feelings for him?

And what about R. E.? Sweet, gentle, loving R. E. Part of me wants to be with him, and part of me doesn't know what to do.

The incessant see-sawing of her thoughts confused Tessa and made her feel disoriented in her own home. A headache started sometime after noon and escalated in intensity until the pounding pain forced her to lie on her bed with a cool cloth across her forehead. Even there the images of Kalluk and R. E. continued.

She attempted to force down a bowl of cereal at dinnertime, but her stomach rebelled. She pushed the bowl away and held her head in her hands. She was close to tears—and she was close to screaming in anger. The thought hit her with such sudden force that she sat up straight in her chair, headache forgotten.

Choice is always a woman's prerogative, isn't it? Even in Alaska? Suppose . . . just suppose . . .

Tessa had coffee ready to serve when she heard Kalluk's unmuffled Jeep snarling up her snowed-in road. The headlights jounced erratically as the vehicle bottomed in potholes and its underpan whacked concealed rocks. She watched out the kitchen window as he wrestled the Jeep, following in the tracks she'd left the afternoon before when she blasted up the drive in four-wheel. Kalluk swung out of the vehicle like a range-hardened cowboy dismounting from his horse. He called Fuzz to him and did something strange: he placed a leather collar around the wolf-dog's neck and snapped a leash to it. The collar was apparently nothing new to Fuzz because he didn't fight or question it. He followed Kalluk in heel position toward the cabin.

Tessa opened the door. Kalluk stopped. The embrace conveyed through his eyes was as real as any he could have accomplished with his arms. Tessa drew a quick breath and stepped back. "C'mon in," she said. "Bring Fuzz."

Kalluk dropped the leash and pointed inside. Fuzz strode in as if he owned the cabin, turned in a tight circle several times in front of the fireplace, and settled on the floor, muzzle resting on his forepaws. His head snapped up as an airplane, flying rather low, passed by. Then he settled once again, his liquid eyes watching Kalluk and Tessa.

"I can't stay long," Kalluk said.

"Oh?" Tessa answered, her voice cautious. "Why not?"

"I got a letter from a community college while we were out. They need me there for a rally tomorrow over fishing and whaling rights for the People. It's important that I go and show support."

"Oh. It's a bit of a surprise, Kalluk. But I realize that it's also what you do."

"Fuzz hates flying, and he hates big groups of people even more. I've been traveling a lot, and it looks like that's going to continue." He waited as if he expected Tessa to respond. When she didn't, he went on.

"I'd like to give Fuzz to you. I can't keep dragging him along with me and locking him up in hotel or dorm rooms. You're the only human other than me he cares about. You told me you're staying in Alaska, that it's your home now. That's great. Fuzz will be good for you, and you'll be good for him. I even brought a fifty-pound sack of the kibble he

230

eats—he takes care of getting his own meat. Will you do it? Will you take Fuzz?"

There was no real decision to make. "Yes. Yes I will." Her words were smothered by the roar of the plane, which was flying even lower now.

Kalluk spoke a bit faster, and his body language was tense, like that of a runner on the blocks awaiting the starter's pistol. "Everything I said on the trail is true, Tessa. How I feel about you, how I want you with me, how I think we'd be together. Please believe that. I know what I proposed isn't your way. I shouldn't try to shove my ways down your throat any more than I allow the lower 48 to do that to the People." He took a deep breath. "I do love you, Tessa. Maybe when I get back from this trip we can get to know one another better."

"Kalluk . . ."

"I'm not asking for a promise or any sort of commitment. Just that you'll consider what I said. If you and R. E. get together, well, I'll have missed out on something great—"

"I made a decision today, Kalluk," Tessa interrupted. "A very important one. I'm changing my life, I'm changing everything about the way I live and think and feel by staying here in Alaska, and that's exactly what I'm going to do. I need to do that unencumbered—learn to live my new life alone before I can live with anyone else. And I'm going to tell the same thing to R. E." Tessa, even through the emotions churning inside her, liked the tone and texture of her voice as she spoke. "You're both wonderful men. I honestly don't know whom I'd choose if I had to choose one of you—but I don't have to make that choice right now, and I won't."

The airplane circled back, and this time flew low enough

over the house to rattle the windows and shake the books on the shelves. The booming of its engine diminished and then entered into a long, droning howl as it eased down toward the road beyond Tessa's cabin.

"I'll be back," Kalluk said. "I gotta go. Jimmy doesn't like to sit around on the road in his Cessna. The highway patrol boys frown on it. Jessie will pick up my ride tomorrow." Then, he was gone, pounding the Jeep back down the long driveway to the road. Tessa closed the door and then leaned against it. She heard the airplane roar again as it picked up speed, and she watched its wing lights as it hurtled through the night.

R. E.'s eyes showed his pain. The store lights in front and on the roof were out, and they sat at a table in the rear of the mercantile, the night light the only illumination beyond a sputtering, small kerosene lamp that seemed to cast more shadows than light. The dark store seemed as vast as a warehouse in the grainy darkness, the shapes of counters and displays and hanging items muted and indistinct.

"I'd hoped that this would be different, Tess," he said quietly.

She reached across the table and took his hand. "Maybe one day it will be. You're a wonderful man, and you're very important to me."

"But you don't want to be with me."

"R. E., that isn't the point. I'm changing my whole life. As of right now, I'm officially an Alaskan. I need to completely accomplish that change, make it on my own, before I can be with anyone. I'll see you just as I always have. I plan to stay in Fairview. I'll find a place to live and some work, somehow. I have money saved. And while I do all that, I want to see what happens between us."

"What about Kalluk?"

"I told him the same thing I'm telling you. He said he'll be back. Maybe he will."

R. E. was quiet for a long moment, thinking. "I can't say I like it a whole lot," he finally said. "But it's better than watching you fly off to Minnesota for good, I guess."

Tessa smiled. "You *guess*?"

R. E. stood and walked to Tessa's side of the table. He bent toward her. "Am I still a hottie?" he asked.

"You betcha."

They hugged.

When Tessa left the store, she started her Jeep and put it in gear—and then stopped and shifted to neutral. She leaned across the bench seat and opened the passenger door. "Almost forgot you," she said.

Fuzz leaped into the Jeep. Tessa tugged the door shut and drove toward her cabin and into a brand-new life.